David McCaddon was born in North Wales and now lives in Cheshire. He is a retired IT systems consultant and has worked in computing for over 46 years, specialising in Law Enforcement Systems Development across police and prisons worldwide.
David is also an award-winning playwright, having had a number of his plays performed over the past 14 years.
His first books in the trilogy *Following Digital Footprints* and *In Digital Pursuit* are fictional crime thrillers set in the north-west of England and North Wales.
The Final Footprint is the last book in the crime trilogy.

TO DAVE & SANDY
BEST WISHES
Dave [illegible]

Dedication

I'd like to dedicate this final book in the crime trilogy to my family – Joan, Simon, Karen, Jake and to my wonderful parents, Nancy and Len. I am just so sorry that my dear dad, whom I think about each day, never got to read this.

David McCaddon

THE FINAL FOOTPRINT

AUSTIN MACAULEY PUBLISHERS™
LONDON • CAMBRIDGE • NEW YORK • SHARJAH

A CIP catalogue record for this title is available from the British Library.

ISBN 9781788489485 (Paperback)
ISBN 9781788489492 (E-Book)

www.austinmacauley.com

First Published (2018)
Austin Macauley Publishers Ltd™
25 Canada Square
Canary Wharf
London
E14 5LQ

Acknowledgements

First and always, Joan and my family for their ongoing support, love and encouragement in writing this trilogy. To Annabelle Hull for always supporting me in my writing projects. A big thank you to Rob Lidiard, Blue Kelly and Wally Wolfe for your help in rekindling those wonderful Oz memories. And a special thank you to all my friends worldwide who have supported me, you know who you are and some of you, of course, may even find yourselves in here somewhere!

Prologue

Singapore Changi Airport – Monday, 4 January, 2016

'Ladies and gentlemen, welcome to Singapore Airport where the local time is 06:30 in the morning and the temperature is 26 degrees.

For your safety and comfort, please remain seated with your seat belt fastened until the Captain has turned off the Fasten Seat Belt signs. This will indicate that we have parked at the gate and that it is safe for you to move about the aircraft. At this time, you may also use your cellular phones if you so wish.

We ask you before leaving the aircraft please check around your seat for any personal belongings you may have brought on board with you and please use caution when opening the overhead lockers, as heavy articles may have shifted around during the flight.

On behalf of Singapore Airlines and the entire crew, I'd like to thank you for joining us on this trip and we are looking forward to seeing you on board again in the near future. Please have a safe onward journey.'

Part 1

Chapter 1

Monday, 4 January, 2016

Paul Arrowsmith (aka Tim Ridgway) seated in business class was one of the first passengers to disembark the Singapore Airlines flight SQ327 from Manchester. He made his way swiftly through the early morning crowds at the busy Changi airport terminal and headed for the nearest business lounge. He had however plenty of time to kill before his onward connection to his final destination – Perth, Western Australia. He had had a change of clothes whilst he had a brief stop at the Manchester airport hotel from the suitcase that his friend Alan had provided him with. He was still desperate to find some new clothes to wear once he arrived in Perth. He had been on the run now for what seemed like months but which was in fact only a couple of weeks.

'Good morning, sir, how can I help you?' enquired the business lounge hostess as she eyed up the slightly scruffy unshaven individual standing before her.

'The name is Tim, erm Paul Arrowsmith,' he replied quickly correcting himself and handing over his onward boarding card and almost forgetting he was now using a new identity. He was tired, would clearly have to watch that and couldn't afford any slip-ups. Tim Ridgway was no more, well for the time being anyway, he was now on the run after his escape from the welsh prison HMP Dinas Bay on the North Wales Coast.

The lounge hostess seemed to inspect every inch of his boarding card before almost reluctantly handing it back to him finally.

'Thank you, sir, that will be fine, please go through to the right, we'll give you a call when your flight is ready for boarding.'

Paul made his way through into the business lounge. He helped himself to a large orange juice from the drinks fridge and took a seat in a beige leather armchair in the corner. Even though it was still early morning, the lounge was bustling with business travellers reading their newspapers and enjoying a quick continental breakfast before embarking on their journeys to the various destinations throughout the world. He looked around still concerned that someone might recognise him and turn him into security but everyone was either engrossed in their morning newspaper, informing social media of their presence in the airport or just catching up on their emails. He finished his drink, decided to go to the bathroom, have a long hot shower and at least freshen himself up.

As he entered the bathroom, he checked to see if there was anyone else in there. The place was empty; he had it to himself. He took the mobile phone out of his pocket and left a quick message via his Dropbox account to his ex-cell mate Charlie who he believed to be still on the run. He then rang the pay-as-you-go mobile number that Alan had given him at the airport but there was no response. Paul Arrowsmith suddenly felt very lonely and somewhat anxious. He then removed the SIM card and proceeded to smash the phone against the granite worktop. He collected the pieces and threw them into the waste bin, he didn't want to be traced but needed to keep his contact numbers. He'd decided he would buy a new mobile phone once he was in Perth.

He grabbed a large fluffy bath towel from the shelf and stepped into the shower cubicle. He stripped off, placed his clothes and towel on the wooden seat and stepped into the most refreshing gush of hot water; he could have stayed in there for hours. On eventually returning to the lounge, he sat back and wondered whether Charlie would have picked up his message from Dropbox as arranged. He was curious as to how he was getting on. He assumed Charlie would now be in hiding in a crofters cottage somewhere deep in the Scottish Highlands. He certainly hadn't realised that Charlie had in fact been recaptured in Glasgow Central Station and was now spending time in the segregation unit back at HMP Dinas Bay. He thought to himself,

As soon as I get to Australia, I'll try and contact Alan again to see if there was any news of him. Little did he know that Alan was also now helping police with their enquiries in the Midshire Police Custody Suite.

***

Richard Ashcroft was driving down the Stirling Highway to his plush smart new offices in Claremont, a western suburb of Perth, Western Australia. He had recently taken early retirement from Western Australia Police after serving some thirty years as an officer. Richard had been a dedicated police officer and over the years had worked his way through the various departments and just prior to his retirement, headed up their High-Tech Cybercrime unit as their Superintendent. It was here that Richard had first hit on the idea to establish his own specialised computer services business. Much to his wife's annoyance, Richard had no plans whatsoever to start taking it easy and relaxing on nearby Cottesloe Beach; that could wait for a while. His wife had been looking forward to long holidays in Europe, cruising to far-flung places and generally enjoying their retirement time together.

With the increase in online crime and the cut backs in resources, Richard however had spotted a possible gap in the services market and he could see the potential for establishing his own IT services business. This was no ordinary computer business however, this was something he'd always wanted to do secretly, establish an independent Cyber Crime Investigation organisation of his own and this had led to the creation of CCI (CC Investigations) Pty Ltd. It was early days yet for CCI and with only himself and his partner, Eric Clough running the business, he had to be careful not to run too fast too soon.

Eric too had recently retired from the force and had joined him in the business venture as a fellow director. They had immediately recruited to date two young systems engineers who had joined them directly from university but now they needed additional resources and in particular someone with a strong proven development experience, someone as Richard would put it *'someone who has been there, been round the block a couple of times and done that ideally in a Law Enforcement environment.'*

Richard parked his Mercedes in the car park and made his way through the smoked glass doors into the plush new offices. Eric as usual was already in the office staring somewhat blankly at his computer screen.

'Good morning, Eric, how's it going? You are looking slightly puzzled. Did you have any luck going through that latest batch of CVs we had received from the recruitment agencies last week?'

'G'day, Richard. Well not really mate, there are one or two candidates that are maybe worth looking at but they either want far too much salary or they don't have sufficient expertise. I'm not getting anywhere with this lot and I think maybe it's time that we looked around for candidates ourselves and placed an advertisement in the local press.'

'I agree, Eric, we can't waste too much time on this one. I'll prepare an advert and see if I can get something published in the local press later this week. We need to move fast though if we are to bid for that all important Watchman project. At this stage, I feel we are still somewhat light in development experience and to be honest, I think as it is, it's badly leting down our proposals.'

***

DC Jack Hodgson had been summoned to attend a meeting with DCI Bentley in the Midshire Police Headquarters. He had just been reinstated following his suspension for misconduct and not carrying out his senior officer's orders during his undercover role in a North Wales prison. This was his first day back in the office after the Christmas and New Year break and he was wondering what sort of reception would await him when he would step into the DCI's office. He woke up at 7 am sharp, made his way quietly towards the en-suite bathroom to avoid waking his wife who was having a well-earned lie in.

The children were still off school for another day. He opened the bedroom curtains slightly on his way to the bathroom and took a quick look at the weather outside; it was snowing. It was not quite blizzard conditions but enough to result in significant traffic delays on the A34 route into the city centre. He thought, *Strange how even a light snowfall affects drivers the way it does in the UK*. Jack decided therefore to take the train into the city and walk the rest of the way to Police HQ. At least that way he would be there on time, the last thing he wanted was another set to with the DCI.

Two hours later, he walked into Force HQ reception.

'Good morning, I have an appointment with Detective Chief Inspector Bentley.'

'Ah yes, good morning! It's DC Hodgson, isn't it?' came the reply from the receptionist, 'can you please sign in. He is expecting you, can you go up to the third floor and I'll ring his PA to meet you at the top of the stairs.'

DC Hodgson signed the visitors' book and made his way to the stairwell. He avoided the lift and made his way up the three flights of stairs and sure enough, there to greet him at the top was the imposing figure of Elizabeth Gilmore who had remembered him from his last visit.

'Good morning, Mrs Gilmore.'

'Good morning, DC Hodgson, you are a bit early for your appointment. I thought last night's snowfall might have held you up a little, but I'll see if the DCI can see you now to save you waiting. He is quite busy at the moment but he is expecting you.'

Jack Hodgson took a seat in Mrs Gilmore's office; it reminded him of the time he had sat patiently outside the headmaster's office when he was a young schoolboy awaiting for a reprimand.

Moments later the as usually efficient Elizabeth Gilmore re-appeared, 'Yes, you are in luck, you can go in now DC Hodgson, the DCI will see you now.'

Jack Hodgson entered the DCI's office and was again not quite sure of what sort of reception to expect. The DCI could be a very moody person and this was the first time they had met on Police premises since he'd suspended him just before Christmas. They had had strong disagreements followed by huge blazing rows on the telephone, which had led to his suspension. Hopefully the mood today would be somewhat lighter and much more amicable.

'Good morning, sir and a Happy New Year to you.'

'Ah Jack, come on in, yes and it is good to see you again. Happy New Year to you and your family, please sit yourself down,' said the DCI, who suddenly seemed to be treating him like an old long lost friend. 'Now firstly please accept my sincere apologies on that blasted business over in North Wales, I am sure you will appreciate that we were all under significant pressure to get to the bottom of everything as a matter of urgency, you in particular of course. Each of us may have said some things in anger we now regret, still it's all done and dusted now and I'm sure you agree it's time for us now to move on.'

Jack took a seat and opened up his notebook. He thought it might be done and dusted as far as the DCI was concerned but despite the huge drugs haul, there was still a matter of a prisoner on the run, Charlie Ellis had been re-captured but Ridgway was still out there somewhere.

'Now, Jack, the reason that I've called you over is of course firstly to apologise to you again personally for what turned out to be a rather messy business. You were in a difficult position and the less said about it, I suppose, really the better. I think in hindsight, we placed you in an impossible situation and I'm sure you will be pleased to hear that your undercover days are now well and truly over, as far as I'm concerned anyway. However, my main reason is to ask you to take charge of a different type of investigation. Something you can get your teeth into. It's a bit of a challenge but an investigation that I think you can excel in, the crime type of which seems to be on the increase particularly in our force area.'

'And what sort of investigation would that be, sir?'

'It's Cyber Crime, in particular ransomware demands.'

'Sorry sir, ransom what?'

'Ransomware demands, I'm sure our High Tech team can give you chapter and verse on it but from what I understand these are a relatively new modern threat. You may have read about this in the newspaper. You know the sort of thing, the scam is built on an ancient approach where a person demands a ransom in return for giving something or someone back, in the case of cybercrime the criminal is a hacker and in return for paying a ransom, he or she will offer the password to unlock someone's own data.'

'Does this thing have a name?' enquired the DC who had started making notes.

'It does indeed, Jack, this particular one we are talking about is known as Cryptosafex. It's based on one of the oldest types of crime in the book, like kidnapping or hostage taking. For example, do you remember in 1932 when Charles Lindberg's baby son was kidnapped and held for ransom?'

DC Hodgson thought for one minute that surely the DCI was losing it and had been reading too many superman comics. He was wondering where on earth this conversation was going.

'Yes, well it's a little before my time sir, but yes I recall that, I think I saw the movie once.'

'Well at one time that was the biggest FBI case in history, but the buggers this time are doing the same type of thing with individuals and organisation's data. It's costing individuals and companies an arm and a leg to get access to their own data. The sods encrypt someone's data and then hold them to ransom for money in exchange for releasing a password.'

'Unless, of course, sir, they have the good sense to keep multiple backups of their data.'

'Exactly, but many don't you know, you'd be surprised. Even organisations think they are safe from this sort of attack but this thing can even access their backup copies that are left online. Do you know, Jack? I think almost gone are the days when a criminal had to go out in the dead of night, the buggers can stay at home and commit crime from the comfort of their own bloody sofa these days. So anyway, I digress, back to the job in question, can you please get along to the high tech crime unit from tomorrow, they could do with someone from CID to run the investigations with them and I said you are just the man. They have an additional problem in their unit, as their senior officer is also off on long-term sick at present so you'll need to be their senior officer on all their administrative matters. I've spoken to your boss DS Holdsworth and he has cleared everything for your transfer. You will as from today report directly to DI Chandler although you will be the senior officer on the investigation, which is known as Operation Unicorn.'

'Thank you, sir, but I'm not sure I have the right level of IT knowledge or for that matter, the seniority. Some of these guys are what I would call Tefal heads you know, they talk their own language!'

'Nonsense, Jack, they need someone like yourself to lead them, someone they can look up to and head up the investigation. Granted they may have all the necessary IT skills but they are not police officers and may lack the essential investigative experience that is required here. I think you are the man with those qualities so there are no problems there. You'll be a good match, they've got a sound team over there. I think you might know one or two of them from the past. A word of warning of course, they are all techies so go easy with them and whatever you do, don't let them bullshit you, old chap. Once they know they can bullshit you, they will keep trying it on.'

'Yes, OK sir, why not. I'll give it a go, in for a penny and all that.'

'That's the spirit, Jack. I'll email them immediately to let them know you are coming over. Oh and one other thing, you mentioned seniority as a possible issue, well you'll be pleased to know that I've recommended you for promotion to Detective Sergeant, you'll be acting of course as a DS until you pass the examinations. I checked with HR and you are already on your way. God knows you deserve it.'

'Thank you, sir. I really appreciate that.'

'Not at all, in the meantime I've got a meeting shortly with Jim Holdsworth to try and work out where our bloody friend Ridgway has disappeared to. That will be all for now DS Hodgson, thank you for calling and I look forward to hearing on how you will be getting on.'

Jack Hodgson had a spring in his step as he left the DCI's office, suddenly he liked the sound of DS Hodgson, *Yes*, he thought, *I could get quite used to that.*

Chapter 2

A Western Australian Government spokesman officially announced today the go-ahead date for Project Watchman, the multi-million dollar government cross-agency pilot project which is designed to streamline the investigation process and fast detection of crime throughout the region. The controversial infrastructure modular project has already been put out to tender. The tender has only been issued to a previously selected list of companies who have been chosen after having expressed an interest in participating in this high profile innovative project. The first module is expected to be implemented by December 2016.

Chapter 3

Paul Arrowsmith had passed through immigration at Perth with no problem whatsoever. He'd completed his immigration card stating he was on holiday [in line with the visa that Alan had arranged for him through the travel agent]. He was still surprised that no one had stopped him but of course, he did have all the right paperwork. He stood patiently at the luggage carousel in the arrivals hall at Perth International Airport waiting for his suitcase to appear. While he was waiting, he couldn't help noticing a large electronic advertisement on the wall for serviced apartments in the centre of the city and thought that one of those would do him fine for a couple of weeks until he found somewhere more permanent.

Soon the conveyor belt burst into life and he watched as the airport beagle sniffed every suitcase as it appeared on the carousel. He thought he had no fears there unless his mate Alan who had packed the suitcase had left him something for the journey. He eventually collected his suitcase from the carousel, made his way past the beagle dog handler and was about to walk towards the Customs Hall and onto the taxi rank exit when he was stopped by an officer and directed to the triage area. His heart stopped and he thought any minute now he'd be directed to an interview room. He had no need to concern himself and after a few simple questions and inspection of his immigration card he was soon on his way again. As he stepped out of the fully air-conditioned terminal building, the heat hit him full on. It was enough to crack the pavements. He'd never felt anything like it, even on his previous trip to Hong Kong. This was a different kind of heat though. It was 4 o'clock in the afternoon and the sun in the January azure sky was blazing down. He approached the first taxi driver on the rank who was talking with another driver whilst leaning against the bonnet of his car.

'G'day, mate! How's it going? And where can I take you on this fine summer's day?' said the driver while cheerily stubbing out the remains of his cigarette.

'I understand there are some serviced apartments on Hay Street in the city centre? Afraid I can't remember the name of them. Can you please take me there?'

'Yeah! No worries! I know the place. It'll be my pleasure, mate! Jump in! We'll have you there in no time at all.'

The taxi driver placed his suitcase in the boot of the car and Paul took a seat in the back of the white Ford Falcon.

'I guess this heat's a bit warm for you poms, mate? Particularly coming from those cold winters you have. I bet you are not used to this kind of weather. We have had another 40c this arvo and most folk have headed down to the beach.'

They set off down the Airport Drive.

'Yeah, I must admit it is a bit warm, but I'm sure I'll get used to it! It's certainly better than where I've come from!'

'And where was that, mate?'

'Erm…Manchester.'

Paul stuttered as he had almost responded with HMP Dinas Bay.

'Ah, Manchester United!' exclaimed the taxi driver.

'City actually,' replied Paul, while wondering why it was that every taxi driver outside the UK always seemed to respond with that line.

The driver then continually bombarded Paul with a number of questions on where exactly he'd just flown from, which airline he was on, what the food was like on the plane, his relatives, the weather in Britain this time of year, the trouble with immigration, the correct temperature for beer, and so on. But soon, to his relief, they were heading past the casino and onwards across the Causeway Bridge towards the city centre.

'Here we are, mate! That will be twenty-eight dollars. You have a great time while you're here. Good location this, mate – not far from the bars and restaurants. You'll have a great time.' They pulled up outside the smart apartment block.

'Great! Thanks ever so much – and please keep the change,' Paul replied as he handed over two twenty dollar notes. The driver thanked him and passed him the suitcase.

Paul made his way into the empty entrance foyer of the serviced apartments to where an attractive, blonde receptionist was seated behind a desk reading the local weekly newspaper.

'Good afternoon, sir. How can I help you?' she asked as she greeted him and placed the newspaper in the desk drawer.

'Good afternoon. I'm afraid I don't have a reservation and I'm hoping you have an apartment that I could rent for, say, about two weeks until I find somewhere more permanent?'

'Yes, certainly, sir. I'm sure we can manage that. Have you just arrived in Australia?' she asked as she started to key in his details.

'Yes, first time here and I'm a bit tired. I've just flown in from Manchester.'

'I'm sure you must be. What name is it, sir?'

'Arrowsmith, Paul Arrowsmith,' he replied, as he confidently handed over a forged company credit card from his wallet.

***

Tuesday, 5 January, 2016

Considering the time of the year the weather was fine over in North Wales with bright blue skies and a fresh crisp feel to the place. Betty Reed was busy in her kitchen wading through the many recipe books she had acquired over the years. She thought it was funny that after all these years of collecting book after book of recipes, she still at times couldn't find the right one she needed for a dinner party. She had a book case full of them. Betty was indeed planning a dinner party for the coming weekend and struggling to find exactly what she was looking for.

The Reed family were a well-to-do family. Her husband, Brian, ran his own successful management consultancy business from their stone farmhouse in Snowdonia, and they frequently entertained potential business clients and friends alike. They had moved here a few years ago when Betty decided to give up her teaching job at a primary school in Stoke-on-Trent. With Brian being able to run his business from almost anywhere in the UK, it seemed sensible for them to move to their favourite holiday destination and enjoy the peace and tranquillity of the lovely Snowdonia National Park.

As she leafed through the endless recipes, she shouted through the open farmhouse window to Brian, who was working in his office in the nearby converted stable block.

'Brian, when you have a minute, dear, can you see if you can find me a recipe online for Salmon Coulibiac. I can't seem to find a single one here.'

'I can't hear you love! Can you speak up?'

'Salmon Coulibiac!'

'For what, dear? Salmon what?' came the reply from Brian as he opened the office window.

'Salmon C-O-U-L-I-B-I-A-C.'

'Will do, dear, but I'm just a bit busy at present. I'll add it to my list of things to do.'

He closed the window, tapped in the search for the recipe, found a couple of possible matches and continued working on the document. He had to finish it today if he had any chance of submitting his proposal and winning the next consulting assignment for the company.

As he continued to type the document he was working on, he hadn't even noticed that his internet browser had crashed and was already activating a silent process.

***

Charlie Ellis had just been allowed out from the segregation unit at HMP Dinas Bay after his prison escape and recapture episode at Glasgow. He vowed never to get involved in an escape attempt again and just wanted to return to serving his sentence. It was Ridgway who had pressurised him into escaping and he had regretted every minute of it. If they had been held in separate wings or even separate cells, it would never have happened, but here he was now, on report, and serving additional time for his role in the whole sorry saga. He had tried to find out whether Tim Ridgway had been recaptured and held in a different prison but he had failed to get any answers from prison officers. Then one day, he was reading the national newspapers and discovered that the Midshire Police were still on Ridgway's trail. The only good thing coming out of it was that Charlie had been allowed to return to his previous prison job, working in the kitchens. A job, which he enjoyed and at least helped him pass the time away.

***

Paul Arrowsmith had been awake most of the night, not only due to a combination of jet lag and the eight hour time difference but also because he had a lot on his mind and had been planning and thinking through his next possible moves. He wondered how long it would be before the police would finally catch up with him.

He was amazed how easy it had been leaving Manchester Airport and then finally getting through immigration at Perth Airport. But of course, he did have all the supporting documentation in the name Arrowsmith, so why should the officials be alerted? Even in Singapore Airport, as he walked around the business lounge, he half expected someone to tap him on the shoulder. Maybe the police assumed that he was still in the UK or possibly even across the Channel in France. He'd heard nothing from his mate, Alan, who had deliberately pocketed a hand-written note with a couple of French hotel telephone numbers just in case he'd been picked up. Yes, it was rather odd, as they had promised to keep in touch. Maybe Alan had now been arrested or was also keeping a low profile?

He decided that instead of just lying there and staring at the ceiling, it was about time to get up. So he made his way across to the en-suite bathroom. Whilst he showered, he thought back to his brief life in prison just a few weeks ago and the grief he used to get in the communal showers there. He quickly got dressed, locked the apartment and stepped out of the block into the street below, which was busy as usual with mid-week shoppers and office workers. He walked down Murray Street in the direction of the shops and restaurants in Forrest Place.

He needed to get himself a pay-as-you-go new mobile, so he called into the small electronics shop down a side street and obtained the cheapest one he could find. He didn't need anything flashy and it would certainly do for now. He then stopped, bought a copy of the local daily newspaper and found a delightful air-conditioned café for breakfast. He took a seat inside, out of the hot sun. He decided he would lie low for a while before looking for a job. After all, with his supply of stolen credit card details and the cash that Alan had given him after the escape, he had more than enough money on him to live comfortably and he didn't want to attract too much attention.

But as he sipped his flat white coffee and leafed through the job pages, purely out of curiosity, he couldn't help noticing the following advertisement:

Cyber Systems Engineer

Due to planned growth, we currently have a new requirement for a ***Cyber Systems Engineer*** *to join our Law Enforcement Systems team.*

We are a new IT company looking for experienced systems development and support people with a proactive approach. Ideally you will have experience of working in a Law Enforcement environment but this is not essential. You will be committed to our exciting development plans and must have strong systems development skills.

A full benefits package including car and share options is available in return for your skills and commitment when you join our dedicated team. This is a unique opportunity to get in on the ground floor of a relatively new company with exciting plans ahead.

Apply with full CV stating experience to Richard Ashcroft (CEO) at CCI Investigations Pty Ltd.

Paul thought for a brief moment. That's all it took! This could be the opportunity he was looking for, so why wait? And it would give him the much needed access to carry out his longer term detailed plans. Without a further thought, he finished his coffee and made his way to the nearest phone box and called the number in the advertisement.

***

Jack Hodgson drove over to Divisional HQ and on entering his old office received the usual banter from one or two of his old colleagues. News had travelled fast of his new technical assignment.

'Bloody 'ell! Welcome back to the real world! I see you are going up in the world and joining the High Tech Unit,' laughed Ted Wilson. 'Would you care to borrow my Janet and John book of Computing for a bit of bedtime reading?'

'Yes, thank you, Ted, for your kind thoughts!' responded Jack putting two fingers up in the air, 'It's always good to know you are thinking about me – and, to be honest, I assumed you yourself would still be reading it. In fact, I bet you are still probably on page one. I think you need it more than me, you ignorant sod!'

Jack started to clear his desk, packing his few personal belongings into a large cardboard box and said his fond farewells to DS Holdsworth and the crime analyst Jean Price with whom he'd been working. Jack had enjoyed working with both of them.

But his last assignment had clearly taken its toll on his marriage. His wife Sue, who did not know the details, had still not forgiven him for taking on the assignment in North Wales, and he was determined never to go undercover again and vowed to spend more time with his family. He drove over to the High Tech Crime Unit, which was now based in the old training school at Broomfields. It was just like old times as he drove into the car park. It only seemed like yesterday that he had worked here in the semi-detached house on Operation Carousel, the stolen vehicle investigations. The High Tech Crime team, however, were housed in a very smart purpose-built IT laboratory just around the corner in front of what had originally been the old parade ground.

Jack parked his grey Volvo Estate in one of the visitor parking spaces and walked across the gravel path to the front door. As expected, the front door was locked and he pressed the intercom buzzer. There was no sign of life whatsoever and for one moment, he thought he might even be at the wrong door.

Eventually, a voice responded.

'Can I help you?'

'Yes, it's DS Hodgson from CID Special Operations.'

'Do you have an appointment?' came the curt response.

'No, I don't need an appointment,' Jack replied brusquely.

'I'm sorry, sir, but this is a high security department and you do need to make an appointment. Everyone needs an appointment to come into this building.'

'Look, I'm not everyone, I am based here from today if you'd care to check your emails!' responded Jack who was now getting somewhat agitated with the welcome he'd received.

He waited for what seemed like hours but it was in fact a few minutes and without any further comment via the intercom, the electronic door lock suddenly clicked and released. He pushed the door open and walked down the spotless corridor to find a spotty youth in jeans and a tatty old polo shirt coming out of a nearby office to meet him.

'I'm sorry about that, sir, but no one has informed us that you were joining us and we were not expecting anyone today. I just checked with HQ and yes, we are apparently expecting you! Afraid there has been some confusion. The main office is just down here on the left. Can I get you a coffee or tea?'

'Yes, that would be good. Coffee black, no sugar, please,' replied Jack. He was keen to forget the experience and thought the communication, or more to the point, the lack of it in the force hadn't changed much.

He made his way into the main office where four more civilians, all casually dressed in jeans, tee shirts and trainers, kept their heads down whilst working across a bank of laptops and large PC monitor screens.

'Good morning, everyone, I'm DS Hodgson! I've been assigned as the senior officer on Operation Unicorn.'

Suddenly everyone stopped what they were doing and looked up from their screens. They all seemed somewhat puzzled to see him. At that point, the spotty youth returned bringing in a tray of coffee and he was the first to speak.

'Sorry, sir, I just overheard you from the kitchen. What is Operation Unicorn exactly?'

'Well, I can see that you have all been well briefed – NOT! Operation Unicorn represents the force investigation cases into the recent Cyber Crime Ransom demands. Now, if you can point me to a desk that is free with a force internet connection, I can get started. I propose that this afternoon at 2pm prompt, we all convene in the small conference room over there. We can then discuss how we can all get along and run this operation together.'

Jack was then guided to an empty desk where he plugged in his laptop, connected to the force network and started preparing his briefing notes from the little information he had already been given by the DCI for the afternoon meeting. He thought, *This is going to be much harder than he had first imagined.*

***

'Brian! Your lunch is now ready. Come and get it as soon as you can or it will go cold. I won't tell you again.'

'Coming now, dear,' responded Brian Reed as he finished typing the last few paragraphs and saved the word document ready for when he returned to his desk later that afternoon.

He made his way across the cobbled farmyard into the large farmhouse kitchen where Betty had prepared a hearty soup accompanied by fresh home-baked granary bread.

'It smells absolutely wonderful, love, and just the thing for a cold January day. I must admit I could eat a horse between two bread vans! I'm starving. What is it exactly?'

'It's your favourite, Brian. It's Potato, Leek and Butternut Squash soup.'

'Excellent. We haven't had that for a while. Just the job on a wintry day.'

'Did you manage to find that recipe for me, Brian?'

'Yes. That was no problem, love. I found a website and I've downloaded it. I just need to print it off. Will do it this afternoon for you when I get back into the office.'

'Wonderful. I need to get down to the shops later and get everything I need ready for Saturday's dinner party. I assume the Gartlands have now confirmed they are still coming. It will be lovely to see them again.'

'Yes, sorry I forgot to tell you, love. We had an email this morning from them and they will be here Saturday evening about 6 o'clock.'

Brian finished his lunch and sat down in the armchair next to the log burner for his customary after-lunch nap. Within minutes, he was fast asleep and snoring his head off in the corner. An hour later, Beryl woke him from his slumbers and brought him a cup of tea. He returned to his office and it was then he was confronted with a message on the screen on his laptop. A message he hadn't ever seen before. A demand for $500 to remove the encryption from every one of his documents!

***

The small conference room was just about big enough to hold the Midshire High Tech Crime team. The room was sparsely furnished with a table, six chairs and a whiteboard on the wall which displayed a drawing of which, try as he might, Jack could not understand either the wording or the diagram. It was like another language, another world and clearly some sort of techie stuff he thought.

'OK chaps, let me get this introductory meeting started and afterwards I'll tell you where I think we are at,' said DS Hodgson. 'I'll be working with you on the investigation of these so-called Ransomware incidents. Clearly, not all of you can be spared to work on this so, first of all, can each of you please introduce yourselves and outline the tasks that you are currently involved with and in particular, if you are already working with any of these Ransomware incidents.'

One by one each of the five civilian support technicians introduced themselves and, as requested, outlined the tasks they were currently working on, their experience and their relevant skills. DS Hodgson soon realised this was one hell of a talented bunch of people he was dealing with here. Clearly, the unit had an incredible variety of high-tech skills such as mobile cell site tower analysis, email analysis and communications data analysis specialists, but not all of them would be needed to work with him on this particular operation. It soon became apparent to Jack, however, that there were two people in particular who would be ideal to work on the investigation with him: Rob Spender, the spotty youth who was a specialist in ransomware software detection and Ian Holden, a systems engineer who also seemed to have all the necessary digital investigative skills.

DS Hodgson didn't waste any time and announced his team immediately, allowing the other three technicians to leave the room and return to their other tasks in hand before he continued with a summary of the incidents to date.

'Now, as I see it, guys, we have had six reported incidents of this over the last two months. There may well be more, of course, which have not been reported to us. Not everyone reports these occurrences, of course. Four of these six seem to have been triggered when members of the public access a particular recipe website. The other two have been triggered by people accessing a false link to some sort of an online betting site. Rob, I'd like you to get in touch with our colleagues in the National Crime Squad to see what they can tell us. You may well have contacts with your counterparts there who can provide some useful additional information. I also want a detailed presentation from you so I can fully understand what we are dealing with here.'

'Ian, I'd like you to contact the anti-virus software providers to get their view on what they see is happening around the UK. I'm sure these incidents are not isolated to our region and the anti-virus guys will have a finger on the pulse as to the trends in this type of incident. I'll set up a case on the system to log all the recorded incidents and occurrences. I'll also speak with the main internet service providers involved to see if they can throw anything into the pot. We'll meet up again on Wednesday at 9 am prompt to discuss and collate everything we have so far. So is everything understood? Do we all know what we are doing?'

'Understood,' came the reply in unison.

Chapter 4

Wednesday, 6 January, 2016

Paul Arrowsmith had decided to take a taxi to the offices of CCI, as he still hadn't become sufficiently familiar with Perth and its surrounding suburbs. He planned to hire a car later in the week and have a good tour round. He most certainly did not wish to be late for this first interview as this was a golden opportunity and he didn't want to waste it. He'd smartened himself up, shaved and also invested in a suit, shirt and tie, together with a briefcase, for the interview with Richard Ashcroft. He'd been amazed how quickly CCI had responded to his phone call and remembered how difficult it had been to find the right job after leaving university in the UK. In the past, he'd filled out endless application forms the majority of which he never received a reply to, or even an acknowledgment. CCI were different. They clearly wanted to see him immediately and they were keen to fill this vacancy.

He stepped out of the taxi and walked through the car park, up the steps into the plush new offices where he was greeted in the reception area by Richard himself.

'G'day! You must be Paul. I'm Richard Ashcroft. Thanks for coming over so quickly. We're in the small conference room just down the corridor here on the right. You found us all right then? Did you have an easy journey?'

'Yes, no problem. I decided it would be easier to take a taxi rather than try and find the place myself because, as you know, I'm still finding my way around here.'

'Yes, I'm sure you are. But you'll soon get used to the area.'

Paul was then led down a glass lined corridor into an office with views to die for looking across the Swan River to a large tree-lined park area. He could see a number of cyclists and joggers taking their morning exercise in the park. He stood in awe of the view as the early morning Perth to Rottnest Island High Speed ferry service glided smoothly and effortlessly past the large patio windows.

'Can I get you a coffee before we start Paul?' asked Richard, pouring himself a cup from the cafetière.

'No thanks. I'm fine, Mr Ashcroft.'

'Please call me Richard! We are all on first name terms here. So, take a seat Paul, and firstly tell me a bit more about yourself. I assume you have brought a copy with you of your latest CV?'

'Yes, I have indeed. Please forgive me, but I can't quite get over the view you have from this window! It is quite spectacular! I've never seen anything quite like it.'

'Yes, it is rather special, isn't it? I sometimes think we take it for granted, you know.'

'It's certainly a big improvement on the view I had back in Manchester,' replied Paul, whilst thinking of the view he'd had most recently, through the bars from his cell window.

Paul reached into his briefcase for a copy of the CV that he had previously copied back in Midshire Police.

He sat down at the large oval glass table and handed over a copy of the CV together with his latest contact details. This was of course the CV that he'd stolen from the real Paul Arrowsmith months ago, when he had first hit on the idea of stealing his identity back at Midshire Police.

Richard leafed through the document, nodding to himself with approval at certain items that had been mentioned. After a few minutes of silence, which seemed like hours, Richard then spoke.

'So, Paul, this is a very impressive CV. You have clearly been busy and had a most interesting career to date. Now, if you will, can you please take me chronologically through your experience after leaving university, together with any special achievements that you think maybe necessary that are not specifically covered here in your CV.'

Paul had to think hard to remember the background of the real Paul Arrowsmith. He'd sat next to him in Midshire Police for long enough when they were both support technicians so he thought he knew him pretty well. He had run through the CV over and over yesterday, back at the serviced apartment block, to make sure he was well prepared for this interview. He had even tried memorising the real Paul's personal data, qualifications, systems experience, hobbies and so on and reeled it off as best he could in good old parrot fashion. There was no doubt about it; this was an impressive CV and as far as he was aware, the real Paul Arrowsmith was still working at Midshire Police. He knew the real Paul had an impressive career track record and had been involved in some pretty significant development projects over the years, which included the development of Holmes, the UK police major incident system.

Richard was clearly impressed. Sitting before him here was someone who definitely had the skills and track record that they were looking for, and what was more, he was available immediately! It was like manna from heaven. There was of course the added complication that this young man had only just arrived in Australia and there would be significant paperwork involved to obtain a visa with work rights, but all in all, he was the ideal candidate for the position and would definitely strengthen CCI's bid for Project Watchman.

Richard continued the interview by describing the job description and outlining the type of work they envisaged he would be working on. Even if they were unsuccessful with Project Watchman, there would be a number of opportunities in the cybercrime area in which they would expect the appointed individual to be heavily involved.

'Well, Paul, having read your CV and heard of your systems experience and the ability to start immediately, I can tell you that you are most definitely on the short list. As I'm sure you will understand, we have a number of other candidates that we need to see but I think we will be deciding by the weekend at the latest so you shouldn't have too long to wait before we make our final decision. In the meantime, do you have any questions?'

'Yes, just a couple, Richard, as you've cleared up most of my questions in your description of the job itself! Firstly, what sort of salary could I expect to be starting on?'

'Well, we would start you on $80k a year and see how things progress from there. We are looking into some form of bonus scheme later in the year, which could possibly lead to some share ownership. It's early days of course in our company, as I'm sure you can appreciate, and effectively you would be starting from the beginning in a company which we think has a very promising future.'

'Well, that is considerably more than I earned with the Midshire Police.'

'I'm sure you understand this is a high profile job, Paul, with a strong emphasis on confidentiality of data but I am pretty sure you would have been subjected to the same levels of security at Midshire Police.'

Paul thought for a minute that it was a good job that Richard didn't know the reasons he was dismissed as Tim Ridgway for accessing the Police National Computer.

'Yes, of course, Richard, exactly the same levels of security I imagine.'

'You implied you had two questions?' asked Richard pouring himself another coffee.

'Yes, my other question relates to Project Watchman. I haven't read anything about this and your outline was useful but this is new to me so can you explain a bit more about what it covers exactly?'

'Of course. It is a proposed pilot at this stage and a good deal of information on this is confidential, as I'm sure you will understand. And it is certainly in the media spotlight. You will need to sign a Non-Disclosure Agreement if we are lucky enough to be awarded even part of this impressive services contract. I am, however, pleased to say we have already been selected as one of the three prospective bidders, following the expression of interest that we submitted last year. Essentially, it relates to the monitoring of considerably more data on individuals and companies etc. For example, at present in WA, we already monitor transactions across all second hand goods stores. I think you call them pawnbrokers in the UK? Every night all transactions in these stores are uploaded to a central database at Police HQ, and are then constantly checked automatically and matched against stolen data from the crimes database. This in itself, as you can imagine, has cut down the buying and selling of stolen goods, and naturally, burglary crimes have reduced significantly in the area. Watchman intends to go much further than this, but how far exactly is being kept under wraps at present.'

'That makes a lot of sense. It seems like a good use of technology to me, but I can understand some people objecting.'

'Good! I'm glad you agree. Not everyone does, of course. Some think it is a step too far.'

He paused.

'Just one more thing, Paul. Can I ask why you left Midshire Police?'

Paul had already prepared himself for this question.

'Oh, that was easy. I really enjoyed my work there, but I had read so much about Australia and I wanted a better quality of life style. Plus, of course, I believe there are more career opportunities for me here than in the UK.'

'Good. Well, their loss is our gain and we are delighted that you have chosen to live here and you are absolutely right: the opportunities for someone like yourself are endless. Well, if there is nothing else, Paul, thank you for coming over, and we will be in touch very soon.'

'Thank you, Richard. I look forward to hearing from you.'

He stood up and shook hands with Richard before leaving.

Paul left the office and started to make his way back to Perth city centre. He was pleased with the way the interview had gone. He clearly didn't expect to be offered the job there and then, but the signals that Richard had been giving him sounded at the least very promising.

He decided to walk to Claremont station up Bay View Terrace and take the train back into the city centre. Once he was back in his apartment, he continued to look through the local newspaper for a more permanent residence. His research into his longer-term plan of action would have to wait for the time being.

***

Brian Reed had been worried sick and had not slept a wink all night. He had spent most of the previous evening trying to clean up the corruption on his laptop and remove the dreaded malware, which had now encrypted all of his documents. At first, he was mystified how the malware had even found its way onto his hard drive. After all, he was only working on a document with no access to the internet. But then he finally remembered browsing the recipe websites. He fortunately had backups of all of these documents and whilst it would still take considerable time to download them he was determined not to pay a ransom to the hackers to retrieve the encryption password.

He grabbed a large mug of coffee and made his way into the office first thing before breakfast. He logged back in and this time he was greeted with a slightly different message, and was now shocked to see that the demand in return for providing the password had now doubled to $1000, and would increase each day. He thought there was no way that he was going to hand over money just to be able to read his own documents and decided to try and sort this lot out himself.

After satisfying himself that his laptop was now clean of the intruder, he sat back and started to retrieve the document copies from his portable hard drive. And that was when he got his second shock of the morning. To his horror, he'd unfortunately left it plugged into a USB port and this too was also corrupted. He had no choice but to spend the next several days scanning in the hard copy documents he had previously printed and tidying them up as best he could afterwards.

'Have you managed to print me off that recipe Brian?' came the voice from the kitchen.

'Not just now, dear. I've got much more important problems on my plate!'

***

Jack Hodgson arrived in the office early on the Wednesday morning. He had decided to base himself in the small conference room rather than using a desk in the main office area. It wasn't a noisy open plan office, far from it, but he felt he needed to be on his own, and it would double up as his meeting room. He called Rob and Ian into the office to go through the incidents that had been reported so far to Midshire Police over the past two months. There was no doubt about it; the Cryptosafex ransomware virus or Trojan was spreading fast and of course, not everyone had yet reported the problem to the Police. Some had even given up and ditched their laptops as a bad job. There appeared to be no specific targets as far as the team could make out.

'So, chaps, can you talk me through your understanding of how this so called Ransomware software gets onto PCs and laptops in the first place and how we can identify the offenders?' he asked as he opened up his folder.

Rob was the first to speak. 'Well, sir, it's like this…'

'No, Rob. Please call me Jack. We won't stand on ceremony here.'

'OK. Sorry! Right – Jack! Well, from what we can gather, a number of websites have been targeted. These are primarily social media sites including cookery, leisure, sports news, that type of thing. Anyone accessing one of these websites will trigger the malware app to be silently downloaded without them even realising.'

'But doesn't their anti-virus software detect this sort of thing?'

'Well, some do, of course, and they prevent it immediately. However, some let it through and detect it later and by then, of course, it's far too late. The bloody things are already running in the background. It gets worse if people just leave their laptops or PC running unattended. This thing finds its way through their entire file system and corrupts through encryption any documents, pictures and so on that it finds. My uncle got caught the other week when he'd visited an online betting site. He left the laptop running and when he came back from lunch every single one of his documents had been encrypted. He ended up binning his laptop!'

'But presumably victims can resort to backups of their files to overcome this? It's just a matter of restoring them?' replied Jack, who was visibly shocked by what he was hearing.

'Yes, if they have any, but you'd be surprised how many people have their backups residing on a portable hard drive which will have been left plugged in. This bloody malware even finds its way on to that. Believe it or not, some users only take a backup once, when they first get their new laptop or PC, and assume that will suffice!'

'So how do we find the offenders? There must be some clues or trail they leave behind?' asked Jack somewhat naively.

'Well, that's the difficult bit, Jack! We really will need to work with one of the anti-virus specialists who are tracking these attacks. It may be possible for us to identify who is behind this particular one. You'd be surprised. On occasion some of these hackers inadvertently leave a clue to their identity, although not always, of course.'

'OK, I understand that, but you mentioned they target primarily social sites, implying there are other targets?'

Jack was now busy scribbling as fast as he could in his notebook.

'Ah! That's the worrying thing, Jack. It's changing all the time,' interjected Ian. 'We are experiencing these attacks ourselves, even on our own Crime stoppers website. At present, we are OK but I think Midshire Police is also possibly being targeted!'

***

Thursday, 7 January, 2016

Paul Arrowsmith still hadn't settled after the long flight from the UK. He had lost track of the last time he'd had a really good night's sleep. Suffering jet lag, he'd been up most of the night, working on his laptop, drinking tea, pacing the bedroom or just watching television. He was just starting to doze off again around 8am when his mobile phone rang.

'Hello, Paul Arrowsmith speaking,' he answered, almost half asleep.

'G'day Paul! I'm really sorry to trouble you so early in the morning. Richard Ashcroft from CCI. I have some good news for you. I'm delighted to tell you that we'd like to offer you the job of systems development programmer.'

This was like music to Paul's ears. He couldn't believe his luck. He'd only been in the country a few days and already he'd landed himself a job! And not just any old job.

'Oh! That's great, Richard! Thank you very much. I'm absolutely made up! What a great start to the day. Naturally, I am delighted and really looking forward to working with you.'

He sat up in bed and rubbed his eyes to make sure he wasn't dreaming.

'I'm sure you are, Paul. Now, look! I know it's short notice, but we'd like you to start as soon as possible. Next Monday, in fact, if that's OK with you?'

'Yes, it is indeed. I'm not doing anything else and can start straight away. But won't I need some sort of work visa or permit?'

'Yes, but don't worry about that I've got my work cut out arranging that for you. We will of course need to start the process of getting you a sponsored work permit as soon as possible, but you can leave all that to us. I'm sure we can sort that out for you. So we'll see you in the office next Monday then?'

'You will indeed, Richard, and thank you once again.'

***

'Well, I think he's still in this bloody country, Jim,' bellowed DCI Bentley down the phone. 'I mean, come on, surely he has to be. He couldn't have slipped away that easily! All ports and airports were on alert. We'd have had some sort of a sighting.'

'I'm not so sure, sir,' replied DS Holdsworth, who was beginning to lose patience with his boss but knew he had to hang on and bite his tongue.

'So what on earth makes you think that?' replied the DCI as he sat back and eased his large frame into the leather chair.

'Well, we've had no official sightings of him, sir, and of course it was a very busy time of the year, with people travelling after the Christmas break. I think he's somehow slipped the net. I mean, surely someone would have recognised him by now and reported it to us if he was in this country.'

'It's a fair point I suppose, but you can only stay in hiding for so long, you know. That works both ways. He could be under our very noses for all we know. So what in your wisdom do you suggest then, DS Holdsworth?'

The tone had changed and Jim Holdsworth knew that when the DCI called him by his rank and surname rather than his first name the pressure was now firmly on him. The two of them normally worked well together but the cracks in their relationship were now starting to show in their efforts to locate the whereabouts of Tim Ridgway after his escape from the Welsh prison.

'Well, sir, I think we have to work out where exactly he could have got off the train. Do we agree that it was probably somewhere between Carlisle and Manchester that he must have got off? We need to get hold of any CCTV footage at each of the stations and from inside the trains themselves and see what turns up. One further thought though, sir, which has been bothering me. Did he actually even get on a train? For all we know he could still be in Scotland or the North of England somewhere. Did he go north with Charlie Ellis? Or maybe he could still be in Carlisle for all we know?'

'You're right, Jim, I had thought of that but I wanted to dismiss that idea. Anyway, I can't spend any more time with this. We need results, and we need them fast. We also need to follow up the possible French connection, those hotel numbers found on Alan Smith when we arrested him. I look forward to seeing what you come up with as a matter of urgency.'

The DCI slammed down the receiver.

Chapter 5

He had just finished typing the last line of the source code on his tablet. He quickly read it over and checked everything just to make sure he hadn't missed anything obvious. It was all there. He then compiled it, attached it to the submit button script and uploaded the amended subroutine to the server.

He sat back in the orange plastic chair with his arms behind his head and laughed out loud.

Soon he would be receiving the first fresh requests for the fifteen digit encryption password and the money would continue to roll into their bit coin account. He thought what a shame that he wasn't in a position to spend it just yet.

***

Richard Ashcroft had just finished putting the final touches to the management summary on their bid for Project Watchman. Although they were seen as the new kids on the block, he felt they now had all the skills and resources they would need in order to offer a viable service to the Watchman team. Clearly, they would have to work hard with whoever the government chose as their prime contractor, but he didn't see that as a particularly big issue.

'Well, that's it Eric. I've just saved the bid document on the network drive. Please cast your eye over it and if you are in agreement, we can finalise the entire document with the changes that you recommended. In the meantime, I'll see what paperwork we need to put in place for Paul's sponsored work permit. I assume you've informed the agencies that we have now filled the vacancy?'

'I have indeed, Richard. They were rather surprised, I can tell you, that we have found someone suitable so quickly, but yes, we shouldn't get any further calls from them.'

'Great! Yes, I daresay they were surprised! We dropped in lucky there. Do you know, I still can't believe our luck, and it certainly strengthens our bid. I suggest that next week Paul familiarises himself with the bid documents and the work we did recently for Evans & Johnson. It will be useful having another support guy on that project. Just to be on the safe side, I will double check his references back in the UK, but on paper he certainly has all the right qualities and skills for us.'

***

Adam Taylor had recently been seconded from the government's IT department and appointed as the director of the Project Watchman procurement. He had called a project meeting to brief the team responsible for the evaluation of the proposals, which were due in any day.

'Guys, now listen up. Next Monday, as you know, we will be receiving all the bids in for the project from the three companies we have previously shortlisted to work with us on the development of the first module. This is a sensitive application, which has proved to be somewhat controversial in the media. The first module will be the monitoring of website company activity, ANPR/CCTV vehicle recording and facial recognition. Can I remind you that we are looking at a number of factors in their proposals?'

'The lowest priced tender won't automatically be the favoured option. I suggest, therefore, as discussed previously, that we will be applying the following weighted scoreboard evaluations, namely:

Experience – 15
Functionality – 30
Innovation – 15
Speed of Development – 10
Project Management – 10
Desirable Options – 10
Price – 10

In addition, we will of course be looking at how each of the companies measure their own capabilities in delivering this. We also need to consider the individuals that each of the companies are proposing for the project team. It is a very important aspect that they propose individuals with a strong track record with relevant experience. Each of you will receive a copy of the proposal documents on Monday afternoon, I suggest we meet back here a week later on the following Monday, the 18th January, to discuss our initial findings. Are there any questions before we return to our desks?'

'Yes, Adam. I have to admit that I'm a bit confused. Firstly, are we looking to integrate this module with the existing systems, such as the crime reporting system, crime stoppers and cash trader applications; and secondly, you don't seem to have put any weighting on integration capability? I mean, some of these ideas may be all well and good but integrating this lot could be a complete nightmare.'

Peter Skelton, the systems architecture consultant, was reading the notes from his laptop.

'Not as yet, Peter. We will be looking to integrate at a later date once all the modules have been awarded. At this stage, all we want to do is just capture the data purely for analysis purposes to see what may or may not be possible in data matching. Remember, it is a pilot scheme to assess the benefits of this approach. Who knows, we might not even reach the integration stage. However, we do need to keep an open mind and identify any potential issues that we could encounter, so if you do see anything that causes you concern, please make a note of it and alert us.'

'I'm still not quite clear on how Project Watchman can assist the state with crime investigations. I mean, I know disc storage is cheap these days but aren't we in danger of capturing data just for the sake of it? We could end up with a right monster trying to manage this lot.'

'Sorry! I almost forgot, Peter, that you missed the internal briefing that we had from the Police last month which covered all of this in great detail, so please accept my apologies.'

'Let us imagine, for example, a situation where the Police investigate say a robbery where jewellery and electronic devices have been stolen. Currently, of course, anyone trying to offload their ill-gotten gains to a second hand store will already have their transactions monitored, but with Watchman we will be able to go a stage further and also automatically receive data, video and images from surrounding ANPR and CCTV cameras in the area at that particular time. These will be supplemented with any face and vehicle recognition matches from other Police databases. Couple all this with automatic monitoring of other databases and you will see that this offers a major step change in Police investigations.'

'Yes, I can see the benefit of that, but I don't understand where the company web monitoring fits in.'

'Ah, well, that is a completely separate process that we are conducting as part of the joined up justice initiative and is primarily for the Tax Office people. The intention will be to monitor any company websites and check for any Directors of companies purporting to claim GST (Goods and Services Tax) who may not even be registered with the revenue. Different kettle of fish, of course. Do you know, you wouldn't believe the number of companies who fall into that, charging for GST and then pocketing the proceeds for themselves!'

'Right, I understand where you are coming from now,' said Peter, who was now nodding in agreement.

'So, Adam, just so I'm getting this straight, are we looking to whittle the three down to two for negotiation, or are we using the process to choose our preferred partner?' asked Henry Jameson.

'I think, ideally, Henry, that by the time we have read their responses we should have identified the preferred partner. But it could surprise us and it may be somewhat closer than we think. We'll have to suck it and see. If we have two preferred bidders, then so be it. It just gives us extra work during the negotiation stages.'

'Well, if there is nothing else, we will call it a day and look forward to seeing what the companies come up with. Thank you, gentlemen.'

***

PERTH, Western Australia – A Civil Liberties group on Wednesday protested in a march in large numbers down St George's Terrace. The protest march was good-natured but held up traffic for almost an hour. They were protesting at the Government plans to monitor data from emails, CCTV recordings and internet access. Frank Carstairs, spokesman for the protest group, openly criticised the pilot scheme known as Project Watchman. He said, "This is a typical case of Big Brother and the public will not stand for it. It will be a complete waste of taxpayers' money. I call on the Government to think again."

In response a government spokesman said, "The pilot scheme, which has now received the go ahead and full backing, is designed to assist investigative agencies with tackling crime and terrorism and is planned to go live later this year."

Chapter 6

Friday, 8 January, 2016

Kevin McNeil had just returned from a successful business trip to Singapore where he had secured a multi-million dollar contract for importing electronic equipment into the Australian market. Kevin was well off, very well off in fact. He had built up McNeil Industries almost single-handedly from what was initially a back street electronic gadget shop over the past decade to be a significant player in Asia Pacific. From his ranch style house, which overlooked the golf course in the exclusive Vines area of Perth, he commanded his empire of wholesale and retail stores across Australia. Kevin was a workaholic and when he wasn't looking for the next big opportunity, he could be found at his subsidiary company buying and selling real estate property throughout WA. What little spare time he did have he could be found relaxing on his brand spanking new 66-foot Luxury yacht *'Pommie Dream'* down at the Royal Perth Yacht Club with his wife Anne and his stepdaughter Karen. Kevin thought the world of his stepdaughter; he'd been married to Anne for eight years and brought Karen up as his very own. His wife Anne had gone through a messy divorce some years back when Karen was only two years old and she had never known her real father who had since returned to the UK. Kevin and Anne had met when she came to work for him in one of his retail stores. It was love at first sight for both of them and Kevin had swept her off her feet proposing to her after only three weeks of meeting her.

Friday was the normal day that Kevin visited the main administration offices of the company situated in Fremantle but today he was somewhat delayed with matters at home. His huge house right on the edge of the superb 18 hole golf course was situated in grounds which spread to well over three acres of immaculately kept garden. The grounds were maintained in pristine condition and had been looked after for the past five years by a local gardener who took great pride in his work.

The gardener however had left recently following an almighty row with Kevin over the refusal of an increase in his daily rates. Kevin had since advertised for a new gardener and was in the process of interviewing the two candidates who had applied. One, a man in his late sixties although very experienced, the old man would have struggled with the size of the gardens; the other, a young man who had recently emigrated to Australia showed much more promise and Kevin decided there and then on the spot to offer him the job which he had accepted.

He drove his Jaguar XF into the car park, parked in his reserved spot and was about to step into the offices when he took a call on his mobile.

'Good morning, Dad, I'm really sorry to trouble you, I know you are busy but are you in a position to talk at the moment?'

'Hi, Karen, yes of course I am, especially for you. I'm just about to go in the office, are you ok, love, is everything alright?'

'Yes, I'm fine. Look, Dad, I'm really sorry to trouble you,' she said repeating herself 'but I'm just letting you know that I'm going over to stay with Jane for the weekend down at Guildford, there is a rock festival on down there which sounds really good. I rang mum earlier she said it would be OK and I should be back all being well on Sunday evening for the usual family dinner.'

'Well, you look after yourself, love, and take care, give me a ring if you have any problems and I'll be straight there to come and pick you up.'

'Of course I will, Dad, I am eighteen now you know?'

'Yes, I realise that but you are still my little girl.'

'I'll see you on Sunday evening then, Jane's dad said he'd drop me back at home so don't worry about picking me up. Bye for now.'

'OK well goodbye, love, and you take care.'

Kevin made his way into his office where his PA Jane Paterson was busy opening and sorting the day's post on his desk. Kevin had fancied Jane from the moment he first interviewed her. He'd tried endlessly to talk her into having an affair with him, wining and dining her but she just wasn't interested and he'd finally given up on the idea. Nevertheless, they had a good working relationship. He tiptoed up behind her and clasped his hands over her eyes.

'Guess who?' he said trying to put on a different accent.

'I know your after-shave anywhere, Kevin McNeil, welcome back.'

'Good morning, Jane and it's another fine day with not a cloud in the sky. I should be out on my boat in this weather not coming in here to slave over a hot desk.'

'Good morning, Kevin, I'm sorry I didn't hear you come in. I'm a bit surprised to see you today to be honest. I thought you'd be resting at home after your trip. Did you have a good series of business meetings? I guess you are a bit tired after all that travelling?'

'I did indeed, Jane, a bit tiring and very busy but it was most productive. If this deal doesn't put us on the map, then nothing will. I'm pleased to say we now have a new exclusive supplier in Singapore. I honestly don't think any of our rivals will get even close to us on the extent of the product lines we will be able to offer never mind the competitive pricing. We have some work to do on additional warehousing space before all this lot starts arriving but it's looking good, very good indeed. It was definitely a trip worth making.'

'That's excellent news, Kevin. Now there are a few messages but first can you give Ken Diamond a call when you have a moment, he has been on several times and says it's quite urgent? There is also quite a pile of post for you this morning. There seems to be rather a lot from overseas which I think you were expecting anyway?'

'Great, yes, thanks, Jane I'll ring Ken before I look at that post. Yes, I'm sure the overseas mail will be the contract and costings I've been waiting for from Singapore. I must say they haven't wasted much time, the documentation has probably arrived back here before me!'

Kevin sat down at his desk and called Ken Diamond on the landline.

'Ken, it's Kevin. I gather you needed to speak to me urgently, is everything alright, what's up?'

'Nothing to worry about, Kevin, in fact it's all good news. Just letting you know that we've made a breakthrough with the online retail website project. We are now ready for the big switch on, we plan to go live on Monday, 18 January. Marketing have already released the advertising, we will be hitting the press and TV at the start of next week!'

'That's fantastic news; it's made my day, Ken, suddenly all the pieces are starting to fit into place. Keep me posted, mate, I must start on this bloody huge pile of post in front me. I'll call you later; we'll maybe grab a spot of lunch together.'

Kevin replaced the receiver and started browsing through the massive pile of paperwork that had built up during his absence over the past few days. As he opened one of the letters, he was disturbed that a rival company Gforce Technologies was once again making him an unsolicited offer to buy his business, the business he had worked so hard for over a decade to build up from virtually nothing. There was stiff competition in the electronics market and already the company had received previous offers to buy him out. The market certainly was not without its enemies and Kevin was not prepared to see his hard work just handed over to someone else so he could put his feet up and retire. Kevin, already a multi-millionaire, was determined to make his first billion. He ripped up the letter and threw it into the waste bin.

***

Saturday, 9 January, 2016

L'Alpe d'Huez, France

The 2016 ski season in L'Alpe d'Huez was now well underway and Monsieur Maurice Vignon, the owner of the 4* Hotel Grand Alpina, was now making the final preparations in readiness for a large party they were expecting from a ski club in the UK who had booked the entire hotel for the week and were due to arrive at any time. Monsieur Vignon had even taken on extra staff to ensure that all the rooms were ready and everything was in place. He had just been advised by the Housekeeping department that all rooms were now ready and he logged into the computer in his office at the back of reception when he received an unsolicited email. He thought at first it was one of those junk emails trying to sell him insurance and he was about to delete it when he noticed it was addressed to him personally by his Christian name. He was curious, opened the email and was totally shocked by its contents. The email was quite specific stating that the hotel computer had just been accessed within the past five minutes and the electronic door system had been hacked and none of the hotel guest rooms could be opened by their key cards.

The email continued to state that if the hotel did not pay a ransom of 2000 euros by midnight then it would be doubled each day until the ransom was finally paid. Monsieur Vignon immediately dashed up to the first floor to check on a number of rooms and sure enough, the key cards had no effect whatsoever. He called in his IT manager who immediately attempted to restore the server to the backup from the previous day but this too failed resulting in a message informing them that the system was now well and truly locked. By now, the large party from the UK had arrived by coach from Geneva airport and after the flight coupled with the three-hour coach journey was naturally keen to get into their rooms.

The situation seemed hopeless as the three coaches pulled up outside the foyer. The noise was becoming deafening with now close on 120 guests waiting to check in and congregating in the reception area. Monsieur Vignon guided them all into the lounge bar and explained that the hotel had encountered a technical fault which should be resolved very soon and in the meantime offered them a complimentary drink from the bar whilst they waited. This seemed to have a temporary desired effect but the situation was becoming desperate and after a further 45 minutes following a number of complaints, he felt he had no option and arranged to transfer the ransom demand to the hackers account. An hour later, the guests finally had access to their hotel rooms.

***

Sunday, 10 January, 2016

Karen McNeil woke up with a mighty throbbing headache from the night before. As she opened one eyelid and looked around, the room looked strange, very strange indeed, this was not her bedroom, she couldn't even remember where she was. She panicked for a moment, she felt as though she had been drugged; here she was in a strange bed in strange surroundings. Gradually she started to piece together where she was, she remembered they had spent all yesterday at the rock festival with her friend Jane and they had certainly hit the bottle very hard. She was just coming round when the bedroom door opened and in walked Jane as lively as ever with a welcoming mug of tea.

'Come on, wakey wakey, sleepy head, you can't spend all day in there, you should be up by now, the bathroom is now empty and the day is young. Remember we've got a lunch to go to in the vineyards and lover boy might be there,' said Jane, opening the blinds and letting in the strong sunlight.

'Oh, shut the blinds quick, who is lover boy and where am I anyway?'

'Do you mean you really don't know? You stayed at my place last night as arranged. Can't you remember anything, not even that boy who was chatting you up, a bit tasty but a bit odd, I'd say?'

'Which boy, I can't remember any boy, you are joking of course!'

'What! You were snogging him as if there was no tomorrow. Don't you remember he came up to you in particular; he seemed to have picked you out? We were dancing in the marquee bar, don't you remember that stupid dance we were doing. He was all over you, he was like a rash. I'll tell you this he must have really fancied you and he seemed really interested in getting to know you. I'm amazed you can't remember him, he kept asking you all those blinking questions.'

'You are joking, aren't you,' she repeated herself; 'anyway, what sort of questions did he keep asking me?'

'It's no joke Karen; you were well and truly gone, completely rat-arsed in my view. I thought you were falling in love with him. In fact, I did get the impression you already knew him although I must say I found him a bit of a weirdo, certainly not my type. Don't you remember he gave us a lift home and he said he might even join us for lunch today at the vineyards?'

'I don't remember any of that.'

'Well, I must admit he did seem more interested in your father's business or maybe he was just curious, you being the daughter of a millionaire and all that.'

'Oh, I feel sick, quick where is the bathroom?'

'In there quick, I'll get you in there before you ruin the duvet.'

Karen aided by Jane dashed across the bedroom and just managed to make it before she was violently throwing up in the toilet.

'Oh God, I feel awful, I just want to lie down and go to sleep. Never again, never again, just leave me here to die.'

'You are making me feel quite ill now Karen. Now stay there, don't move, I'll get you a glass of water.'

Minutes later, Jane returned with the water, Karen was now as white as a ghost; she was flaked out and fast asleep on the bathroom floor.

***

'So do we have any more news on our friend Ridgway yet, Jim? It's been nearly a week now since we last had a sighting, surely someone has seen him?' asked DCI Bentley impatiently.

'We do indeed, sir,' replied DS Holdsworth, 'Ridgway most definitely caught the Manchester train from Carlisle and we have CCTV footage of him or someone who looks like him leaving the train at Manchester Airport. We believe he may have stayed in an airport hotel overnight and we also have an image of someone who looked like him in Terminal 2 checking in at the Singapore Airlines check-in desk first thing in the morning.'

'Great, so where is he now?'

'Well that's just it, sir, we are not quite sure.'

'You are not quite sure!'

'Well there was only one Singapore Airline flight on that day but no one with his name on the passenger list; clearly it's possible he may have checked in under another name, if it was him, of course. He was clearly helped by someone to ensure that he had all the necessary paperwork and possibly the luggage for the flight. There were 400 people on that flight, we are currently looking to try and identify each one. I'm afraid, sir, it's going to be quite a task.'

'Bloody 'ell, is that it, are you quite sure that it was Ridgway that had actually left the train?'

'Well almost, sir, we are doing our best here and we are short staffed as you know, some of our officers are still on their Christmas break.'

'Almost! Bloody almost, now correct me if I'm wrong, sergeant, but you keep using the phrase "*someone who looks like him*", well it's not good enough, is it him or not? Much as I wouldn't mind the trip, we can't afford to go on a wild goose chase to Singapore!'

'Well, we are not sure at this stage, sir, but there is something else which could be of value. You will recall that we arrested Alan Smith, the café owner in Manchester shortly after we lost Ridgway up in Scotland.'

'Yes, I know that, what of it, he's still in custody. He's not telling us anything we didn't already know.'

'Well someone was trying to reach him yesterday, sir; we received a call on his mobile which we now have in our possession of course. The call was from an international location. It may be nothing of course and possibly a co-incidence but I think it's connected. We have also informed Singapore Police and we are trying to obtain the CCTV footage from Changi International airport.'

'Well, good luck there, have you seen the size of the place? Well, some 200,000 passengers a day pass through Changi; you'll have a few sleepless nights and lots of overtime on that one!'

'Yes, sir, but not all of them arrive off the flight from Manchester and we should be able to pick up the CCTV recordings just from the arrival gate.'

'It's a fair point I suppose, so it could be that Ridgway has finally made it out of the country, keep me informed and let me know when you have a definite sighting and I mean a definite sighting, not a definite maybe!'

***

The Sunday roast dinner in the McNeil household was always a special family affair, the one time in the week that the three of them sat down together at meal times. Karen had now returned from her wild weekend at the rock festival and was now feeling considerably better.

The family sat down for dinner at 6pm prompt as they had done for years.

'So how was the rock festival, Karen, you haven't said much about it since you came in I must say?' enquired Kevin as he finished carving the joint at the table.

'It was really good, Dad, well from what I remember of it anyway. Some great local bands, I think you would have enjoyed it. There were all age groups there, something for everyone.'

'No time, love, I'm still too busy with the business at present, maybe next year. So did you meet anyone of interest or was it a case of dancing round your handbags with Jane?' responded Kevin sarcastically as he handed out the dinner plates.

'Well yes, there was as a matter of fact, a boy who I quite liked. We got on really well apparently.'

'Apparently! Can't you remember Karen?'

'Well vaguely, Dad, I did have too much to drink, I'm afraid, but I can remember dancing with him. He was supposed to join us for lunch but couldn't make it.'

'Really, I can feel a romance in the air, Karen McNeil,' said Anne as she entered with the gravy jug from the kitchen.

'No, don't be silly. It's nothing like that, Mum, we were only dancing and he seemed more interested in dad's business than me.'

'Did he indeed and what was his name. I hoped he behaved himself with my little girl?' asked Kevin as he opened the bottle of Shiraz.

'Ah well that's it, Dad, I don't know but he was very nice. He was very polite. I think you'd like him. I'm hoping he will contact me, he has my phone number.'

***

Monday, 11 January, 2016

Paul Arrowsmith took the 08:37 train from Perth railway station for the short journey down to Claremont. Thirty minutes later, after a brisk walk down Bay View Terrace, he walked into the CCI offices bright and early, smartly dressed in his new dark grey designer suit, white shirt and polished black shoes. Yes, he was definitely ready for his first day in the office. As he entered the office, Richard was there to greet him. He gave him a warm welcome and introduced him to the small team.

'Come into my office for a minute, Paul, I have something for you,' said Richard as he led him into his office and handed over to him a new mobile phone, laptop and network login instructions.

'Now you should have everything you need here, Paul, but let me know if there is anything else you require. I suggest you work from a desk in the open plan area. It might be that once Project Watchman starts, you will probably have to be based at their project offices in Adelaide Terrace rather than here but that shouldn't be a problem.'

Paul took a seat at his desk by the window overlooking the magnificent Swan River and following the instructions he logged into the CCI office network for the first time.

Ten minutes later, Richard reappeared from the computer room and handed him a large pile of documents, which had just been freshly printed off the printer.

'Right then, Paul, it's straight in at the deep end I'm afraid. Now I suggest you first start off by reading this little lot, this is the tender document and our associated bid response which has just been submitted for Project Watchman. You will see we are bidding for just the design and the initial development phase of the pilot project at this stage. Let me know if you have any problems with any of it, if we win it you will be one of our key players on the team in helping us to deliver it. I would like you to make notes and maybe we can meet up later to discuss any issues you may have with any of it. I'll be back later but just shout if you need anything. Oh and by the way, every day is dress down day in this office so unless you are on client premises, please feel free to leave the suit behind in the wardrobe.'

Paul sat down and studied the documents in great detail and could see that the project if implemented although controversial could deliver huge benefits in crime detection. He sat and gazed out of the window watching the ferryboats and the leisure crafts slowly gliding their way down the river to Fremantle. For once, he felt he now had a project he could really get his teeth into and finally allow him to show off some of his development skills. There was a small matter of course that the bid needed to be won first.

***

Albert Lewis was an agile 65 years old pensioner who ran the neighbourhood watch project in the Midshire Police Cheadle area. Albert had taken early retirement ten years ago following a lifelong career working on the railways. Albert had never married and when once asked why he'd never married he'd replied in a broad Mancunian accent, "*I don't understand women and as far as I can gather, a wife doesn't come with a manual. When they do, I might just be interested!*"

Since retirement, he had spent most of his time working in his allotment, the location of which he kept as a closely guarded secret, in Albert's eyes anyway. Truth is most of his friends and neighbours knew where the allotment was and they didn't really care where it was anyway, as long he provided them with fresh vegetables on a regular basis. When he wasn't attending his allotment, he could be found walking his Yorkshire terrier named Pip. Albert could be seen most days walking down the many avenues on the housing estate he lived in. Albert was a typical nosey parker, regularly peering into people's gardens and driveways. Pip gave him the opportunity to stand and stare into driveways and gardens. He'd volunteered as the neighbourhood watch liaison officer shortly after retiring and there was nothing that Albert Lewis missed, nothing, whether it was a gang of new workmen working on someone's house or a courtesy car in the driveway when their car was in for repair.

Yes, in Albert's eyes, he was the perfect neighbourhood watch person who constantly sent in his observations to the Crime Stoppers website. Anyone searching on the crime stoppers database for the mention of Albert Lewis would find pages and pages of hits. Yes, Albert Lewis was Midshire Police's best customer or worst depending on how you looked at it. This particular morning, he powered up his trusty old desktop computer, which had certainly seen better days. He logged into the Crime Stoppers website as usual, he needed to inform Police of a suspicious vehicle parked outside his neighbour's house. He filed the details and pressed the submit button and went off to the kitchen to make himself a cup of tea. By the time he'd logged off later that day, every document and photograph he held on the computer had been secretly encrypted awaiting payment to release the password.

***

'We've been targeted, Jack!' exclaimed Rob Spender as he burst into the office.

'What! Tell me you are bleeding joking of course?' replied DS Hodgson as he got up from his desk.

'It's no joke I'm afraid, boss, this is really serious, our IT department have had to take down the Crime Stoppers website, someone has somehow managed to get into it and left the Cryptosafex Trojan embedded on the main submission page. It's offline at present but anyone that had registered a crime or incident over the weekend could well have found they have also been hit with it. We are in the process of restoring it and we should be able to bring it back online this afternoon. We have had a load of complaints from the public saying their PCs and laptops have been subsequently infected and are now blaming us for it. Oh and by the way can you please call DI Chandler urgently? He called you earlier this morning demanding an update on the situation.'

'That's all I bloody well need, I bet old Bentley has already been onto him and probably would have expected me to have sorted this out by now. OK, Rob, leave it with me and I'll get onto Phil Chandler first.'

Rob Spender left the office and closed the door behind him. Jack Hodgson sat down for a minute, gazed at the phone and thought about calling the DI.

He'd worked for DI Phil Chandler before on a couple of major incidents together and they had always got on very well together. Phil was as sound as a pound and enjoyed a beer or two, something he certainly had in common with Jack Hodgson. It had been a while since they had last met face to face. But this was not a good start in his new post and he thought it's no good putting the phone call off any longer than need be and so dialled his new boss.

'Good morning, sir! This is DS Hodgson. I gather you wanted to speak to me.'

'Yes, good morning, Jack. I take it you have heard the news that we have been targeted?'

'I have indeed, sir, all being well we should be in a position to…'

'So, what in god's name are we doing about it?' interrupted the DI who was also clearly under some significant pressure himself to provide answers and a solution.

'Well sir, we will have the website back online this afternoon apparently, cleaning the data up will take a bit longer of course.'

'But have we managed to trace the offenders behind this?'

'Not yet, sir, that's easier said than done and it's early days. We have a meeting later this morning with the anti-spyware company who we are partnering with. I should be able to give you an update later on today.'

'Well thanks, Jack,' replied the DI who by now was softening his tone somewhat 'I'm sure you will be aware that I've got the DCI on my back with this one, give me a call when you have something concrete to tell me.'

'Well, there is something else, sir.'

'And what's that?'

'They've also encrypted some of our own crime and incident reports on crime stoppers, they have also demanded a ransom to decrypt those!'

'What! Oh that's all we bloody well need, get this mess sorted out and quick, Jack, otherwise you and I will be making a trip to Force HQ and I'm afraid the book down the back of the trousers won't help one little bit with this one!'

'Yes, sir,' responded the DS but by now the line had already gone dead.

***

The three proposal packages arrived separately that morning by different couriers at the Project Watchman Office within fifteen minutes of each other and well before the official deadline for responses. None of the companies bidding were prepared to take any chances of a late delivery and then be automatically disqualified from the evaluation process. Adam Taylor instructed the administration staff to time and date stamp the deliveries, issue receipts to the couriers and distribute the copies immediately to each member of the project team. He then took his own set of documents into his office, poured himself a large coffee and sat down to work through each of the management summaries. Two hours later, it was quite clear that without getting into the actual detailed responses, two were well outside their budget and one in particular stood out by miles.

***

Alan Ravenscroft had just completed the accounts for the previous month. Ravenscroft Data Services, based in Wilmslow, Cheshire, specialised in payroll applications and although they were a small company, they were very successful with a large number of clients based throughout the UK. Alan was just about to leave the office for a spot of lunch with a client when he received an international phone call. Normally, he would let it go to the answering service but he was curious and decided it could be important so he took the call.

'Good morning, Ravenscroft Data Services.'

'Good morning, can I speak to Mr Alan Ravenscroft, please?'

'Yes, speaking.'

'Good morning, Mr Ravenscroft, my name is Richard Ashcroft, we haven't met before but I have been given your name as a reference by Mr Paul Arrowsmith who has expressed interest in joining our company. I gather Paul used to work for you a few years ago. I wonder is it convenient at the moment to discuss the reference with you now?'

'Yes, it's fine, Mr Ashcroft, but I am in a bit of hurry as I do have a lunchtime appointment. As a matter of interest, where are you calling from? There seems to be a bit of a delay on the line and I noticed it's showing as an international call.'

'Yes, sorry, it shouldn't take too long. I am calling from Perth, Western Australia, my company is CCI, you probably haven't heard of us as we are relatively new.'

'I see, no I'm not familiar with your company and I hadn't realised Paul had even emigrated. He worked for me for about two years before he joined Midshire Police a few years ago where the last time I heard he was doing well there and was very settled. He's a great guy; nice personality, very capable and his IT skills and knowledge are, I must say, second to none. I'd have no hesitation in taking him on again. We couldn't afford him, I'm afraid, and he needed to move on and advance his career. It was sad really as he fitted in with us very well and would have gone on I'm sure to be probably a director in the company. What do you need to know exactly, Mr Ashcroft?'

'Well I have no doubt as to his technical skills, was he punctual and how did he perform in front of clients?'

'Yes, on both accounts, he was a role model to our other staff. A great, support guy and our customers constantly praised him. They specifically used to ask for him. I'd have no hesitation in recommending him. It was a sad day for us when he left the company but as you know you can't stand in anyone's way when they wish to further themselves.'

'I agree, well that's excellent, thank you, Mr Ravenscroft for your time, you've been most helpful. I really do appreciate your help with this.'

'No problem at all, Mr Ashcroft and please pass on my best regards to Paul when you next see him.'

'I will indeed, he is certainly enjoying life down here.'

Alan Ravenscroft replaced the receiver and sat back thoughtfully in his chair. Strange, he thought that Paul Arrowsmith would go all the way to Australia to work, as far as he could remember he had a huge fear of flying.

***

Tuesday, 12 January, 2016

'I really can't wait much longer, Anne. I've got a stack of work piling up on my desk. He promised he would be here first thing yesterday to start on the garden and he still hasn't bloody well turned up. What is the matter with people? Bloody unreliable, that's what they are. He didn't leave a phone number. In fact, all I know is his first name, I think he said it was Phil.'

'Well perhaps he's ill, Kevin, and he couldn't get in touch with us,' said Anne as she cleared the breakfast table.

'He had our phone number for gods' sake, completely unreliable some people, bloody timewasters. I'll have to advertise all over again. I thought we had this lot sorted, and in the meantime, the grass needs bloody cutting and the borders need weeding. I'll have to have a go at it myself tonight, bloody nuisance as I'm far too busy in work to be bothered with this lot.'

'Calm down, dear, you mustn't get yourself all worked up. You know it's not good for your blood pressure. We'll soon get another gardener; there are plenty of people who will be interested in this.'

'Well, anyway. I can't hang around here any longer I'm off to the office. If he rings, call me on the mobile.'

Kevin jumped in his car and set off to the office. On the way down the freeway, he decided to call a friend of his, Gordon Alison, a private detective. He'd known Gordon for about five years. Gordon had bought surveillance equipment from him and from the moment they had met, they got on well together. They had also played golf together on the course near to Kevin's property.

'G'day, Gordon. It's Kevin McNeil, long time no speak.'

'Hi Kevin, it's good to hear from you and if you are after another game of golf, forget it,' joked Gordon, 'You beat me well and truly last time.'

'No, I need a favour, Gordon. My stepdaughter Karen, I think, is being followed by a young man. I don't have any details and to be honest, I could be worrying unnecessarily as there may be nothing in it. He seems to have been asking her all sorts of questions. I don't have his name, I'm afraid. You know where she works, I wonder could you see if there is anything untoward and let me know.'

'Yes, no problem, Kevin, leave it with me and I'll get back to you with any news, in complete confidence of course.'

***

'We've drawn a complete blank, sir?' said DS Holdsworth as he walked into the DCI's office.

'You are not serious! What do you mean a complete blank? I can't believe we've not got anything back from Singapore yet.'

'Well, sir, we had assumed that Ridgway actually caught that flight to Singapore and...'

'How many times have I told you sergeant, remember the old ABC mantra in CID – **A**ssume nothing, **B**elieve Nobody and **C**onfirm everything. It's served me damn well for almost twenty-five years, now never forget it. Anyway, what did the CCTV recordings tell us? There must be boxes of those somewhere.'

'Nothing, zilch. I'm afraid sir, if he was on that plane, he must have been on it under a different name. To be honest there isn't a single image from any of the video frames that we can positively identify as being Ridgway. I'm pretty sure he made that flight from Manchester but that's where the trail ends.'

The DCI shook his head in disbelief and DS Holdsworth waited for his moment.

'I'm afraid there is something else, sir?' said DS Holdsworth almost reluctantly and standing back as if he was lighting the blue touch paper.

'Oh god, break it to me gently, sergeant!'

'We understand the plane made a scheduled stop at Munich to refuel and take on additional passengers, as far as we know it is possible he could have even left the flight there!'

'Oh shit, this is getting worse, so you are saying he could be anywhere in Europe as far as we know?'

'Yes, sir I'm afraid so, we are doing our best I assure...'

'I despair. I assume you have already informed Interpol and Europol?'

'Yes sir, Ridgway is already on their wanted list.'

'Very well, Jim, stick with it and update me when you have at least some positive news,' replied the DCI as he reached for the Paracetamol in the desk drawer.

***

Jane Paterson was hard at work preparing the consolidated sales forecast from all the McNeil retail branches in Australia. Over the past decade, Kevin McNeil had established several major retail stores throughout Australia and he'd kept a watchful eye on every one of them by receiving regular weekly reports. Every week the stores would submit their individual sales and forecasts for the month ahead. If any store failed to make their targets, he was personally onto them straight away, sometimes visiting them unannounced. Jane had just taken Kevin in a coffee, she'd noticed he wasn't in one of his best moods and decided to just place it down on the desk and leave him in peace. She was just putting the final touches to the latest report and was about to email it to Kevin and the other directors when she received a phone call.

'Can I speak to Kevin McNeil, please?

'I'm not sure whether he is available right now. I think he maybe still in a meeting. I'll check, who shall I say is calling?'

'My name is Lance Smithson of Gforce Technologies.'

'Just one moment, Mr Smithson, I'll see if he is available,' said Jane as she placed the call on hold.

'Kevin, it's for you, it's a Mr Smithson from Gforce Technologies. Shall I tell him you are engaged at present?'

Kevin thought hard for a moment, he was not in the best frame of mind to deal with this but then decided to take the phone call anyway.

'No, please put him through Jane and hold any other calls until I tell you.'

'Kevin McNeil, how can I help you?'

'Kevin, my name is Lance Smithson, we haven't met before but I am the CEO from Gforce Technologies. I was wondering if you had received my latest letter.'

'Yes, I know exactly who you are and I've just received your letter but I can tell you now, Mr Smithson, before you start, we are not interested in any takeovers, mergers, partnerships or shared opportunities with your company. Quite clearly, we are competing in the same market for the same business and have been for some time. At the moment, we are beating you out of sight on most deals, you may have noticed that. Our business is not for sale and to be honest, Mr Smithson, your unsolicited letter has been filed with the other letters you have sent in the appropriate place, the waste bin, so if you don't mind, I have a lot of work to get through today. Thank you for calling, goodbye.'

Lance Smithson was astonished that his offer for both companies to work together had been treated in such a way. He clearly had misjudged Kevin McNeil and it was now time for Plan B to be put into operation. After sitting back and thinking for a moment, he picked up the phone and called his chairman.

Chapter 7

Monday, 18 January, 2016

The Project Watchman proposal evaluation team had all arrived in the office early. They had been hard at work comparing their notes from the three proposals that they had received last week. Each one of the team members had been busy studying the proposals and making their own relevant notes and questions on the final bid responses. Adam Taylor, the Project Director was now summarising the bid situation at the close of their meeting.

'So, gentlemen, I'll be quite honest. I wasn't looking forward to this part of the project but I must say this has proved to be an interesting process and somewhat easier than I had first thought. Anyway, I believe we are all now agreed on furthering discussions with the potential preferred company. I stress potential as we of course still have a lot of discussions to go through first. We have all had time now to read the documents and the responses to our tender, which are well laid out.'

'Henry, can I once again congratulate you on your splendid idea of including a questionnaire and self-marking system, which has certainly made life easier for us all in assessing their responses. As discussed and agreed we start negotiations with our preferred partner first thing tomorrow morning. Judging by your evaluation clearly the preferred company has understood and addressed all of our functional requirements and they appear to have the right calibre of staff to work with us in developing this important first module. We are not, of course, dismissing the other proposals at this stage far from it but rather focussing on this particular one. Please do not, under any circumstances, inform the other two bidders that we have a preferred option at this stage. It may turn out that we may well require further meetings with these companies as part of the evaluation process.'

***

A week had gone by since the Midshire Police Crime Stoppers website had been hit by the ransomware Trojan. Cleaning up the data on the Crime system had taken some time and the IT team had worked around the clock but everything at least was now almost back to normal. The force High Tech crime unit had also managed to produce a list of the members of the public whose reported incidents had been affected and each had been contacted in turn to re-enter their incidents. One or two had been annoyed at the inconvenience of re-entering their crime reports and had threatened to write to the Chief Constable but on the whole most had been very sympathetic and understanding. Ironically, most of the users had been unaffected, as their own anti-virus software had detected the offender before any damage could be done on their own PCs or laptops.

The High-Tech crime team was now in the process of examining the code that had been planted on their website.

'So guys, do we have any clues from the embedded code you have found?' enquired DS Hodgson who was due any day to provide an update to DI Chandler.

'Nothing as such yet, Jack. It's pretty basic to be honest, certainly rough around the edges, pretty amateur really. Although, we think we have spotted something we have seen before on a hacking attack to a local bank. It's coded of course but the lines of code and the format seem to match almost as if it's been copied from another program. We have updated the National Cyber Crime Unit with our findings as it may well match with data from other attacks that we are not aware of.'

'You mentioned a local bank, Rob, which one was that?'

'The Swallow National Bank, it was aimed at their head office website, sir.'

***

The board of Gforce Technologies normally got together every three months. But Lance Smithson had decided he needed to call everyone in to attend an urgent special meeting to inform them of the progress, or more to the point, the lack of it on their hostile bid to acquire McNeil Industries. The chairman, Frank May, a smartly dressed dapper little man stood up and was the first to address the meeting.

'Good morning, gentlemen,' he said tweaking his neatly trimmed moustache, 'Firstly, can I thank you all for attending this special board meeting which has been called at such short notice. I know you all have busy diaries and have other important activities to be getting on with. As you know, the only item on the agenda today is the takeover approach we have made to McNeil Industries. So without further delay, I'll ask Lance to update us on the progress so far. Lance, the floor is now yours.'

The chairman returned to his seat and a red faced Lance Smithson stood up to address the six men sitting around the table.

'Thank you, Mr Chairman, well as you know we have written several times to Kevin McNeil to try and arrange meetings with a view to us working together. I wished I could provide you this morning with some good news but I'm afraid it's not good at all. Despite several friendly approaches to McNeil, we have failed to enter into any meaningful discussions or dialogue on even possibly working together never mind taking them over. Last week, I also called Kevin McNeil personally to discuss how we might work together, and quite honestly, I got an earful off him. He even slammed the phone down on me!'

'I can assure you, gentlemen, we have looked at a number of various options and Kevin McNeil who owns some 80% of the shares is simply not interested in parting with his business.'

'And in the meantime, our share price continues to fall while McNeil goes from strength to strength winning hand-over-fist business deals in direct competition against us,' interjected Jeff Bradley, the group financial director.

'That's correct, Jeff, he consistently undercuts us, buying the business if he needs to. At the same time, he has built an impressive list of clients,' replied Lance Smithson who was clearly rattled by the interruption.

'So what exactly are we doing about it?' replied Jeff Bradley, 'I mean you only have to look at today's papers and you must have seen the constant advertising on the TV. McNeil are everywhere, you can't even open a newspaper without reading either an advertisement or news article on a new business contract they have won. Their PR machine is in overdrive. In the past six months, we haven't won a single bloody contract Are we just going to sit back and let them win everything in sight, what on earth are our overpaid sales guys being paid for exactly?'

'Now hang on a minute, Jeff, that's completely unfair, we are working flat out for these contracts, it's almost as if McNeil has bloody access to our bid material and for that matter, our pricing database. He is constantly undercutting us, what do you expect us to do?' shouted a red faced Jim Walker, the group sales director who looked as though he was about to burst.

'Gentlemen, gentlemen, let's please keep this at least civilised. We are all adults here, we won't get anywhere by shouting across at each other like children,' retorted Frank May who was trying to keep everyone calm and level headed, 'Shall we discuss this in a calm and professional manner? Can I suggest we take this conversation offline? We all need to get our thoughts together and regroup tomorrow morning to agree how we can best deal with this. But before we do disperse, Lance, I have just two questions. Firstly, can I ask you personally to bring to the table tomorrow a suggested proposal on how you see us moving forward? Secondly, I gather you were going to approach an ex-employee of McNeil to come and join us to try and gain an understanding of what is going on in there, how did you get on with the recruitment of this individual?'

'Well, Frank, I did exactly that. We have approached a young man who apparently had an axe to grind with Kevin McNeil for dismissing him a couple of months back. He's an ex-sales support guy and he impressed us with his knowledge of the market. We have taken him on three weeks ago in our sales department as a bid support guy. But to be honest, he's not really come up with anything useful at this stage. His name is John Edmonds and to date he hasn't told us anything we didn't already know about the company. Jim and I plan to speak with him again later today.'

'Something is still troubling me, Lance, can I just ask you something?' interrupted Alan Langtree, the Director of IT shaking his head.

'Yes of course, go ahead, Alan, what is it that's bothering you?'

‘Well, how do we know this guy we have taken on isn’t still working for McNeil?’

‘Yes, fair point Alan, fair point,’ responded the chairman thoughtfully before Lance could even muster a response.

***

Paul Arrowsmith had taken the opportunity to visit several rental properties in the area. He had spent some time leafing through the local newspaper for potential properties and mapping out their exact locations. This had proved somewhat difficult at first as he still hadn’t got to grips with the actual distances of the various suburbs. He decided he would hire a car and had spent most of the day driving around trying to get to know the surrounding area. He’d been very tempted by a beachside villa at Cottesloe overlooking the magnificent Indian Ocean before finally settling on a third floor fully furnished apartment on the Esplanade in South Perth, handy for the city and train service into Claremont if needed. He had to constantly remind himself however that he wasn’t here on one long holiday and he was there to do a job. A job he’d been thinking about for quite some time.

The South Perth fully furnished apartment was just what he had been looking for. It had spectacular views across the Swan River to the city and Kings Park from the lounge window. In short, it had everything he needed, even including a large balcony where he could sit, have a beer and relax after work. It was perfect, whenever he needed to go over to the city, he could even watch from the patio window for the ferry leaving from the fabulous new Elizabeth Quay in the city. By the time it had crossed the river, it was just enough time for him to stroll along to the Mend Street pier and catch the return crossing. He decided he would pay the apartment owners six months up front in cash and had arranged with them to move in over the coming weekend, just in time for Australia Day.

***

Tuesday, 19 January, 2016

Richard Ashcroft and Eric Clough travelled together that morning to the Government offices and parked Eric's silver 'E220' Class Mercedes in the Murray Street multi-storey car park. Armed with their bid documents, they took the short walk across to St George's Terrace to the government project offices. At this stage, all they were expecting was to have the opportunity to present their bid and answer any initial questions that the project team might have. They were well prepared having anticipated most of the likely questions they would encounter. They had been surprised to receive the phone call so early on in the process asking them to attend the meeting this morning, which they had just received as they were closing the office at 6pm the previous evening.

They were, however, in for much more of a surprise. They took the lift to the third floor, stepped out into the hallway and rang the doorbell. Within a couple of minutes, a very nice young lady met them, asked them to sign in and escorted them down a corridor and towards a long open plan office area. She guided them through the open plan area into the conference room and introduced them at the doorway closing the door behind her.

Seated already around the conference table were Adam Taylor, Peter Skelton, and Henry Jameson who neither Richard nor Eric had met before.

Adam Taylor rose from his seat and was the first to speak.

'Good morning, gentlemen, please come in and take a seat. Thank you for coming over at such short notice. We do appreciate you will have considerable other business activity and time is precious to you.'

At this point, Richard Ashcroft and Eric Clough became somewhat slightly nervous. They assumed they were about to be told that they would no longer be considered for the project together with a list of reasons for rejection of their bid. In fact, Eric was almost ready to get back in the lift and head for the car.

'Firstly, can I introduce you to our project team?' he continued, 'I am Adam Taylor, the Project Director and to my right is Peter Skelton, our technical design authority. Sitting next to him is Henry Jameson who deals with all legal and administration matters on the bids. Clearly, we intend to expand the team as the project develops, as I'm sure you will understand.'

'We understand perfectly, Adam,' smiled Richard, 'and it's good to put faces to the names that were in the tender document.'

Richard watched patiently as Adam Taylor opened the CCI proposal folder in front of him and took out a hand written note.

'Secondly, can I thank you for a very impressive response to our tender document? It was most thorough; you clearly have a great understanding of the requirements and the objectives we are aiming for. I'm sure your background as police officers will have helped you enormously with this proposal. We also note you must have put considerable work into your response and that is also appreciated. Also, we are delighted with the interesting innovative suggestions you have put forward in progressing Project Watchman, there are certainly ideas in there we hadn't even envisaged and will certainly put forward to the solutions team.'

Eric was waiting for the '*But*' to follow and he prepared himself for the worst, *Here it comes*, he thought.

Adam Taylor continued, 'At this stage and in all confidence of course, I must point out that we would like to formally open preliminary discussions with your company with a view to signing contracts next month.'

For one moment, Richard Ashcroft and Eric Clough were both shocked and excited at the same time. If they were hearing this right, they were the preferred bidder.

'However, we do need a period of further discussion before we finally decide and award the contract to the successful partner.'

Richard Ashcroft was slightly disappointed that they wouldn't be officially told whether they were successful at this stage. But he realised that these things didn't happen overnight and took considerable time.

'We have a number of questions we would like to ask you. Firstly, can you confirm that the team members you have specified in your proposal will be actually available for the entirety of this project?'

Adam Taylor was wise to this and had seen this once too often when a tender had been submitted with an impressive list of project members with world-class CVs and then to be told after the contract had been signed that those people were no longer currently available.

'Yes, we most certainly can,' replied Richard Ashcroft, 'we believe the success of this project will come down to the skills of the team players and as you can see we have great confidence in the team we are putting forward. We believe our team offers you both strength and depth with their experience and track record in developing comparable systems.'

'And can you confirm who will be the project manager from your side to ensure that everything goes according to plan?'

'Yes, that will be myself, Adam,' replied Richard Ashcroft, 'as you can see from my own CV in the appendix I have fulfilled that role over several projects when I worked for the Police Service.'

'Do you not consider that this will maybe conflict with your duties as the Managing Director of CCI?' piped up a stony faced Henry Jameson in a somewhat arrogant fashion.

'No, I don't see that as a problem. It is our intention that if we are successful with our bid then Eric would take over my other day to day duties to ensure that I can focus 100% on Project Watchman.'

'Excellent, Richard, well thank you both for coming over. I am sure we will probably have some other questions to ask you during the week but we will email those and we would appreciate you also responding by email so we have an audited trail. Can I please ask you not to discuss this meeting with anyone? I am sure you understand.'

'But of course, Adam, we quite understand and we look forward to hearing from you,' said Richard as the two men made their way out of the office to have a well-earned pre-celebration drink.

***

Wednesday, 20 January, 2016

The board of Gforce Technologies had re-convened to discuss their next move in acquiring McNeil Industries. Lance had been up all night working on a plan, which he would need to put forward for discussion and agreement by the board directors. He was getting desperate now, they were losing so much business to McNeil that something radical and even unethical had to be done and fast. Frank May once again chaired the meeting and asked each of the directors in turn to firstly summarise the situation as they saw it from their own point of view. Each of them felt it was now time for serious alternate action and they had to work fast, in short, they could not afford to lose any further contracts. After each one of them had made their point, it was Lance's turn. He finally stood up and over the next half hour presented his strategy and proposal to his fellow directors.

'Well, gentlemen, as you know we have tried everything in our power to team up with McNeil without success, he is not budging one single inch. You will also be aware from our regular forecast business meetings that the government funded Project Watchman has now been given the official go ahead and we expect this eventually to culminate in a multi-million dollar tender for hardware, camera technology, electronics etc. Can I remind you, gentlemen, that this is our type of business? This is what Gforce was set up for in the first place all those years ago.'

'I also don't need to remind you that we are probably at a crossroads in the company's existence. This is clearly the type of business we need to win; it is our bread and butter. Personally, I think we are at that stage and pardon my French but it's shit or bust from here on in! However, what you may not be aware of is a much smaller government contract, which is currently out for tender for 100 laptops. My plan, therefore, is this…'

Lance Smithson went onto cover in detail his proposed plan.

'So are we all in favour of carrying out Lance's plan?'

Six hands shot up immediately and voted all in favour of the plan.

'Excellent, gentlemen, then there is no need for me to cast my vote, your proposal is granted,' remarked the Chairman as he signed off the agreed plan and handed the paperwork to his secretary.

Saturday, 23 January, 2016

Paul Arrowsmith checked out of the serviced apartment block using another one of his forged credit cards. Whilst it was very comfortable, he'd only seen this accommodation as a temporary arrangement and needed to find a more permanent location. He'd been careful on the use of this particular credit card which was not in the name of Arrowsmith but in the name of a company whose details he had obtained prior to his arrest. He'd made an early decision that whilst he was using Arrowsmith's name, he would only use his CV identity. He saw this as just borrowing his career identity and couldn't see any harm in it. Any card transactions would however be in the name of the company credit card he had stolen months ago.

He made his way quickly down Hay Street through the many shoppers, turned into London Court and turned left onto St George's Terrace. As he turned right onto Barrack Street, the huge gust of wind hit him full on and took him somewhat by surprise. He'd read somewhere that Perth is considered to be the third windiest city in the world and it certainly felt like it at times. He made his way down the street to the new busy ferry terminal at Elizabeth Quay and obtained his ferry ticket from the machine on the pier. It was a Saturday morning and he was surprised how many people were using the ferry service so early on a weekend although of course it was the height of summer and ferries were busy with tourists bound for Fremantle and the nearby island of Rottnest.

He didn't have to wait long before the South Perth ferry arrived and he followed a large group of tourists on board who presumably were going across to visit the Perth Zoo. He stepped onto the ferry with just a suitcase and no other belongings to his name. The ferry boat made its way slowly across the river dodging one or two of the small catamarans en-route which were clearly outside of their restricted water zone. Ten minutes later, he was met as arranged at the entrance hall to his new apartment block by the owner Linda Hartley from the real estate agent, a delightful lady who handed him the keys.

Linda then asked him to sign the acceptance and inventory forms before she drove off clearly with a busy schedule ahead of her. He thought I didn't even have time or the chance to ask her any questions but she was clearly very trusting. He took the lift to the third floor, entered the apartment and dropped his suitcase onto the bed before stepping out onto the large balcony. The panoramic views across the Swan River to the city were quite magnificent. Although it was daylight, he could already imagine the view at night with Perth's skyscraper office buildings all lit up across the evening sky.

He thought it ironic that almost a month to the day he had been staring out at a very different scene, looking across to a stormy Irish sea through a barred window. He thought back to the tiny cell where he had been finalising his escape plan from the prison in North Wales. Paul quickly unpacked his suitcase and placed his toiletries in the en-suite bathroom. He now needed to stock the empty kitchen and refrigerator from the nearest supermarket, which was conveniently situated around the corner on nearby Mends Street.

He took the lift to the lower ground floor and stepped out of the apartment building onto the Esplanade. The day was bright and sunny with a very warm pleasant temperature of 30c. The breeze had dropped somewhat but was still relatively cooler for the time of year, nevertheless, very comfortable. Just forty-five minutes later, he returned with his bags and unpacked his shopping in the beautifully equipped and spotless kitchen. Paul decided he needed to get to know the locality in a bit more detail and returned to Mends Street to have a coffee and croissant at one of the local cafés.

As he sat outside sipping his coffee, he reflected on his situation. Yes, he would be very settled here, he had dropped on a good well-paid job, great accommodation, a location to die for and soon he could start working on his plan. The plan he'd spent years thinking about which had lain dormant for all this time, stored in readiness at the back of his mind. But one thing he'd failed to notice was the man across the road in the Windsor Hotel who was videoing and photographing his every move.

***

Monday, 25 January, 2016

With Australia Day looming, a number of Gforce employees had decided to make a long weekend of it by also taking the Monday off. The sales office was much quieter than usual. Lance Smithson and Jim Walker had however agreed to come into work to finish their sales proposal for the latest government laptop tender. The bid needed to be submitted by close of play on Wednesday, 27 January. There was no way they were going to miss the deadline.

Jim had also asked John Edmonds, the ex-McNeil Industries employee to come in and work on the final document with them. They had been working right through the weekend and John wasn't too happy working through it. But at least it paid the bills and he badly needed the overtime. The three of them sat around the conference table in the small meeting room discussing the state of play with their bid document.

'Well, Lance, we are in a pretty good position, the management summary is now written. I personally am reasonably happy with it but I'm not too happy with the final pricing discount that we should offer the government on this one. I mean I would hate to lose this contract if we don't offer them a reasonable discount. I don't need to remind you that McNeil will be targeting this and going in at rock bottom to stop us on this one,' said Jim who was struggling with the cost summary figures.

'I agree with you, Jim, I think this one is particularly important to us. You could say it's a sprat to catch a mackerel as my old dad used to say. I think we should buy the business and go in at say cost minus 5%. We can always recover the loss on the next big one. I'm sure the board would understand our motives for doing this as they will be demanding answers if we are unsuccessful. Let's set it to that, I'll sign it off and take any flack I get from our finance people. Jeff Bradley will hate it of course but I can deal with him afterwards. John, can you please run those figures through the sales spreadsheet and let me know the bottom line. I have a real good feeling about this one. McNeil won't know what has bloody well hit him.'

'It sounds good to me, Lance. I'm sure even McNeil can't get down to these levels unless he's bidding inferior products of course,' exclaimed Jim as he set about the rewrite of the costing summary.

'I agree, Jim, I'd be bloody amazed if we lost this one to him, I mean how low can you go,' remarked Lance as he winked at Jim.

Tuesday, 26 January, 2016

Australia Day

As it was a national public holiday, Paul had decided to have a long lie in and an easy day. He was well over his jet lag and now getting a decent night's sleep. He'd slept soundly throughout the night, the king-size bed in his new apartment was extremely comfortable, certainly compared to the metal bunk bed in his old prison cell.

One of the things he also didn't miss from the prison was the loud blaring music heard from the other cells. He finally arose from his slumber at 10:30am and walked out onto the sun-drenched balcony. Still in his underwear, he stretched his arms out and was staggered with the sight immediately in front of him. There on the freshly mown lawns between the apartment blocks and the Swan River were a number of partygoers. They were already gathering in readiness for what looked to be a big picnic, a very big picnic.

They had already set up their gazebos in what was a designated alcohol free zone and the BBQs had been fired up ready for brunch. Paul was amazed at the number of people who were now setting up their chairs and tables on the grass. This was the first time that Paul had ever witnessed Australia day and he was impressed with the efforts that went into it. The Aussies certainly knew how to celebrate their National holiday.

Out on the river, he could see three large pontoon platforms, which had been presumably towed there overnight and were now being prepared with fireworks for the night ahead. In the distance on the roof tops of the skyscraper buildings, he could also see men working presumably to prepare the fireworks for the grand finale. Soon hundreds of small crafts of every description came sailing under the narrows bridge. They had moored on the river in readiness for the huge fireworks party later that evening.

Paul spent the day watching the large crowds and he had a ringside seat, actually the best seat in the house. As he sat there later that night enjoying the skyworks, he thought back to how he was surrounded by people in prison and here he was 9,000 miles away now on his own. He had the balcony all to himself but whilst everyone else was out there enjoying themselves with friends and family, he suddenly felt that he was the loneliest man on earth.

Chapter 8

Monday, 15 February, 2016

'Can you believe it? He's actually fallen for it!' said the voice on the telephone.

'I didn't think he'd go for it but that's great, we can now go for the next stage in our plan, do you have everything in place?'

'Yes, pretty much everything is now in place, all the arrangements are already in hand, it's cost us next to nothing so far and we now have the location and assurance that the goods have actually arrived.'

'Can you trust them?'

'Oh yes, there is no problem there.'

'But we also now know who we can and cannot trust.'

'We do indeed, that's for certain, agreed.'

***

Kevin McNeil and Ken Diamond, his Group Sales Director were out celebrating with lunch at a high class city centre restaurant having won their latest government contract for the supply of 100 laptops. Ken had worked with Kevin as his right hand man for the last seven years and had helped him build the company to the level it was at today. Ken was on the ball, a ruthless, devious but likeable sales guy and nothing would stop him from winning business. Ken would work endless hours nurturing his sales contacts, providing hospitality, wining and dining them on company expenses and always positioning himself ready for when any tenders were eventually issued. The wining and dining however had taken its toll somewhat. Ken who was once a slim athletic sports fanatic and a committed cross-country runner was now well overweight. Yes, Ken liked his food and in particular, the wine that accompanied it.

'Can we please have another bottle of the 2012 Leeuwin Estate Margaret River shiraz mate?' shouted Ken to the efficient restaurant waiter who was lurking and waiting patiently in the background. He could see a large tip coming his way if he played his cards right.

'Certainly, sir,' came the response from the waiter who started to go off to the wine cellar.

'Steady on, Ken, go easy, we are not making money on this one, in fact we are losing on it,' replied Kevin McNeil as he nodded across to the waiter to continue with the order in any case.

'Yeah, I realise that, Kevin, but you have to admit we are now well placed for the likely equipment coming out of that new Watchman project. I've heard that the tender for that little beauty will be awarded anytime in the next two months and we are now nicely positioned.'

'I think you are totally wrong there, Ken. They are only now awarding the service contract for the development phase. It will be a while before they start procuring any hardware. They won't even have identified what it is they need until the designers have done their bit.'

'Well, I still think part of the equipment tender will follow on very shortly, Kevin. I know for a fact they have the money in this year's budget and we have to be ready for it. We need to be well placed in readiness.'

'Agreed, if it all goes to plan, which it should do, we are certainly well placed when that tender comes out. I mean our latest advertising and marketing program with regard to the online retail website will raise our profile massively and is also doing us the world of good. Do you know we are fast becoming a household name? We couldn't have planned it better if we'd tried. Now I've already arranged to call off the delivery of those high specification laptops from our supplier in Singapore for this latest contract. The laptops should be with us in our Fremantle warehouse by this Thursday morning. Gforce Technologies must be pig sick losing this one, I can tell you. They thought they could buy this one and at this rate they will probably have to start laying people off and we can pick up some of their employees. Do you know I think maybe it's our turn for a hostile takeover bid for their company, Lance, whatever his name was, will be pig sick!'

'It sounds like John might have to re-join us!' laughed Ken out loud who had failed to notice the young man in the next dining booth who had been listening in on their entire conversation.

***

Friday, 19 February, 2016

It was pitch black; the two men parked their beaten-up old Holden Ute down a sidetrack, just off the old main Fremantle to Rockingham Road. They waited and checked their watches, minutes later they nodded to each other. They locked the vehicle (not that anyone would have stolen it) and made their way on foot down the unlit lane past a row of trees and alongside the two-metre high razor wire fence. The first man took out the wire cutters from his pocket and snipped open enough of a hole for them to climb through. They slowly and carefully made their way in the shadows across the empty car park in the direction of the goods receiving bay. The second man carried a small hold-all containing two torches, two power packs, a pair of scissors, some rolls of tape and a couple of USB memory sticks, they didn't need any specialist tools for this job.

This would be one of their easiest jobs yet. They had watched over many nights the comings and goings of the lone security guard on duty and found that at 2am precisely, he was always back in his gatehouse cabin at the main gate having his early morning coffee and sandwiches. You could set your clock by his eating habits. They edged quietly alongside the main warehouse building until they found the ground floor toilet window, which had been left unlatched as previously arranged. They climbed through the window and made their way across the dimly lit corridor into the goods received area. To their surprise, the warehouse had its emergency lighting on, just enough for them to find their way round without the need for torchlight. It didn't take them long before they found exactly what they were looking for. There they were stacked up in a corner, one hundred cardboard boxes still on pallets freshly arrived from the Far East labelled for the attention of the state government.

The first man swiftly re-read their instructions they had been given to make sure they had understood them. They quickly opened up the first box, and found the laptop within, and powered it up. There was sufficient power as expected to meet their needs, they plugged the memory stick into the USB port, downloaded the contents onto the laptop and powered it off immediately. They resealed the box and soon got into a routine repeating the process for 32 other boxes working individually as fast as they could. They made their way back out and were out of the building before the security guard had resumed his patrol at 3:30am. Half an hour later, they were back in the van.

'This is the first job I've ever had to do without nicking anything, in fact leaving something! It's money for old rope,' laughed the driver as they sped off down the highway. Ten minutes later, they were back at home counting the $50 notes in the package that had already been left for them as arranged.

***

The evaluation of the three Project Watchman proposals had taken slightly longer than first anticipated with the company background checks slowing the process up, however, discussions with Richard Ashcroft and the CCI team had gone very well indeed and the Government project team were now ready to sign contracts with CCI for Phase 1. They had arranged for both the CCI project team and government representatives to join them on the Friday afternoon at 2pm promptly for the formal signing and post contract celebrations. Richard and Eric arrived five minutes early at the government offices and were shown through into the large conference room where Adam Taylor and his small project team were already waiting together with a number of civic dignitaries.

As they entered the room, they were each offered a glass of champagne and canapés. They made their way to the small gathering at the front of the conference room. Richard could see a number of distinguished guests, some he recognised and a few new faces that he didn't. There was one man in particular however, who stood out from the small crowd, a tall distinguished looking and sandy-haired gentleman with glasses, probably in his early sixties dressed in a smart grey two piece suit. Richard had seen him before somewhere but he couldn't quite place him.

'Good afternoon, gentlemen, and welcome to the Project Watchman contract signing ceremony. I'm sure like us this is the moment you have all been waiting for,' said Adam Taylor as he reached out to shake hands with the two men from CCI.

'It certainly is, Adam, we are really looking forward to getting started on this project I can tell you,' replied Richard Ashcroft as he and Eric continued to sip their champagne.

As they were talking, the man in the grey suit with glasses made his way over to meet them and Adam was quick to make the introductions.

'Can I first introduce you to one of our other guests today? This is the Head of Government Services – Phil Pleasance who is responsible for the entire project. Phil, this is Richard Ashcroft of CCI and his co-director Eric Clough who I was telling you about earlier.'

'I'm pleased to meet you both,' said Phil Pleasance enthusiastically, 'I read all about your company CCI this morning and I'm delighted that you have been awarded the contract. We too are waiting anxiously for the start of this project. As you can imagine, we have a number of ongoing projects at present in Government Services but this one is considered in my eyes to be the innovative flagship. Ever since I became head of the department about five years ago, it's been one of my personal ambitions to see this particular project delivered and I'm naturally delighted we are at last on our way. We believe we are the first certainly in Australia with this type of development and I am sure you can imagine I have made some enemies with this one. We believe, however, this could offer a huge breakthrough in crime investigation. Once the results start coming in, I think people will change their mind. A lot of eyes are upon us as I'm sure you understand, we need to make this a big success.'

Richard Ashcroft was unsure of the protocol and didn't know whether to call him Phil or Mr Pleasance, so instead opted for his full Christian name.

'I agree, Philip, and it's good to meet you too, we are ready for this. I can tell you as retired Police officers, we too can see the benefits and we are also looking forward to seeing the outcome of this. We see it as a major step change in crime investigation.'

'Well without further ado, gentlemen, let's get this contract signed and let's hope it's the first of many,' said Adam enthusiastically opening up the black leather folder and picking up the gold pen placed before him.

Richard Ashcroft and Adam Taylor then proceeded to sign the paperwork to the scene of flashing cameras, the sound of great applause and the subsequent clinking of champagne glasses.

Chapter 9

Thursday, 25 February, 2016

Anne McNeil had been busy packing the overnight bags for their long weekend break that the family had recently planned. With no money problems whatsoever, you would have thought the McNeils would have been constantly on exotic holidays and jetting off to far-flung places but this was far from the case. Kevin McNeil was a workaholic, it had been a miracle that he'd finally given in and even agreed to take just a few days off.

He was work mad and it had taken great pressure from both Anne and Karen who would constantly nag him into taking a well-earned rest. A weekend break, which was well overdue. Finding a slot in Kevin's diary however had been difficult, to say the least, and he had insisted that he would have to be back at the office on the Tuesday morning for a series of important meetings. They were just about to leave the house when Kevin received a call on his mobile.

'Hi Kevin, it's Gordon Alison here, you asked me to check something for you.'

'Ah, Gordon, yes did you discover anything?' asked Kevin trying to be as vague as possible with his wife and step daughter listening in the hallway.

'Nothing worth worrying about, Kevin, just thought I'd let you know.'

'Thanks, Gordon, thanks for trying, will be in touch,' replied Kevin closing the call.

'Who was that dear?' enquired Anne McNeil.

'Oh nothing dear, just checking on a supplier.'

So with everyone now ready and packed up, they loaded the bags into Anne's silver Range Rover Vogue. The three of them were soon heading down the Reid Highway on their way towards the Royal Perth Yacht Club where Kevin's luxury yacht was moored. On arrival at the private marina, they were greeted at the gatehouse by the security manager Bruce Graham who came out to the vehicle personally.

'And which far flung place are we off to this time, Kev, taking the yacht on a world cruise perhaps, just popping over to the Philippines or pootling around in the harbour?' joked Bruce as he opened the security barrier for them.

'World cruise, I wish, Bruce! No, this is just a few days relaxation on Rottnest, mate. The world cruise will just have to wait for now,' laughed Kevin as he drove through to the marina car park. He continued through the car park and parked adjacent to his yacht. The yacht looked absolutely magnificent, gleaming in the bright sunshine and had been spotlessly maintained by the marina staff.

After loading up the *'Pommie Dream'* and having completed all the necessary on-board checks, Kevin fired up the powerful engines and very soon they would be heading down the Swan river and out towards the nearby idyllic island of Rottnest.

'I still can't believe you've agreed to these few days together, Dad,' exclaimed Karen as she brought her mum and dad up a welcome brew from below.

'Me neither, Karen, but don't get used to it, and remember I have to be back on Tuesday afternoon at the latest for a sales meeting,' shouted Kevin as he guided the vessel expertly down the swan river and eventually out across the Indian ocean towards the island.

'Yes, you've told us enough times, Kevin, now just sit back and relax love. Enjoy it, after all it's not often the three of us can get away together like this. We should do this more often you know. I mean what's the point in investing in this beautiful yacht and not using it,' said Anne as she sat back and sipped the hot tea.

'Yes, you're absolutely right, love, what is the point, let's try and enjoy more time together. Do you know I've quite forgotten how relaxing these trips can be. Now sit back whilst I open this beauty up,' replied Kevin who was now sitting back on the pristine white leather seat and was at last starting to enjoy the short break.

Just Sixty minutes later, they had dropped anchor in the crystal clear waters of Porpoise Bay at Rottnest Island and were now preparing to go ashore for dinner.

***

Bill Hancock had worked for the WA Government IT department for the last five years. He had started as an IT apprentice straight from school and progressed as far as he could within the support section. He was now responsible for implementing and connecting any new desktop hardware to the government network across Police and all emergency service users. These were exciting times for the support team with several ongoing projects as a result of increased government funding. The small team of support technicians were now working flat out to keep up with the pace of project rollouts. Bill was just getting himself a coffee from the vending machine when his mobile rang.

'Bill, it's Alex Goodman here, I've had the Superintendent of the Police HR project onto me and we need to start rolling out those new laptops that we've received as soon as possible. Can you please drop everything and get onto it right away? I promised him we could do fifteen of them today so sorry to drop this on you. I gather all of the laptops have already been delivered there and they need them commissioning urgently. I'd like to get them up and running today if at all possible. I owe you one.'

'No worries, will do, Alex, I'll just finish what I'm doing and get straight onto it.'

Bill Hancock had a good working relationship with his boss Alex and didn't waste any time, he drank his coffee and then made his way across the building through the labyrinth of corridors to the force HR department. Sure enough, the entire consignment of boxes were there waiting for him, addressed for his personal attention and he set about unpacking the first box. He removed the laptop from the packaging and having connected all the cables he powered it up. But all was not well, something was definitely not right. It powered up much faster than he expected for a start.

He was in for a shock and horrified to see that instead of getting the familiar windows login screen he expected he was now receiving an unusual screen display, a screen he hadn't seen before. This was not, however, a demand for money to un-encrypt any documents on the hard drive. But instead, a rolling display was showing him a series of expletive hard core pornographic images, the likes of which he'd never ever seen before and certainly didn't wish to see again. He quickly powered off the laptop and started to open the other boxes. The next one and the ones after that were the same.

***

'So how many of these bloody laptops are affected?' shouted Alex Goodman down the phone.

'Well, I've opened ten of the boxes at present, three of them seem alright but five are all displaying the same hard core pornographic images when they are booted up. The other two seem to be locked out and won't boot up at all. To be honest, I don't trust any one of them.'

'So can these images be deleted easily, Bill?'

'Well no, it's a lot worse than that I'm afraid, Alex. It's quite a drama really as the screens are completely frozen and the operating system is locked out, they are completely unusable in their current state. We could rebuild them of course but that will take considerable time and effort.'

'So who on earth was the supplier who provided these and how long have we had the bloody things?'

'Well, I've double checked the paperwork. They are all from that single consignment which we ordered earlier this month through McNeil Industries, it was a recent order. We have had deliveries from the company before without any problem whatsoever. They only arrived here a few days ago and I'm sure no one has tampered with them after they arrived here in the HR department. They were still sealed up.'

'Have you had any joy contacting anyone at McNeil Industries yet?'

'I certainly have, Alex. I managed to speak to their despatch department earlier. They can't explain anything and couldn't understand it. They said they had only received the batch of 100 laptops a few days before they were despatched to ourselves and they have never been out of their sight. They had been stored in McNeils Fremantle warehouse. They are as baffled as we are and have sent their sincere apologies.'

'I bet they do, well I'm afraid we will have to escalate this little lot and get McNeil in here himself if needed to meet with the head of government services. This has to be reported, heads will definitely roll on this one and it won't be mine.'

Bill Hancock thought, *No and it won't be mine either.*

***

Paul Arrowsmith had been working on the software development of the first module on Project Watchman and he was really enjoying it. He got on well with most of his other team members but he had somehow got off to a bad start with Peter Skelton, the Technical Design Authority on the project. Paul had criticised one of the specification documents as being over kill for its purpose and Peter had taken great exception to this. For once, however, Paul was at last working on a project he could really get his teeth into without breaking the law and enabling him to demonstrate his skills as a programmer.

He was now based at Adelaide Terrace working alongside other civilian staff on the changes required for the Automatic Number Plate recognition software. Paul had started the programming modifications that would be required on the speed cameras. In the final rollout of all phases, each speed (or safety camera as they are preferred to be called) throughout the city would, in addition to performing its normal speeding role, be modified to automatically capture the vehicle details together with an experimental face recognition capture from within the vehicle. This latter aspect was already proving troublesome in system trials particularly if the vehicle windscreen or the camera lens was dirty. The trial of the system would only be implemented on a number of selected camera positions. Route data from the satellite navigation systems on the vehicles would also be collected and downloaded automatically at force HQ.

Once all of this data was captured, it would then be stored and consolidated in the Project Watchman database for later investigation should it be needed.

Richard Ashcroft was delighted with Paul's work and he visited him on a weekly basis to make sure he had everything he needed and to review the project status; but to all intents and purposes, Paul Arrowsmith was now an integral part of the Police development team and didn't need managing. Paul was in his element particularly as he now had unaudited access to a wealth of other data most of which he had no right whatsoever to view.

***

The McNeils had changed for dinner and were taking the short walk around to Thomson Bay to the restaurant. It was a balmy summers' evening and it was just starting to go dusk; in the far off distance, the early evening lights of Fremantle and beyond could be seen twinkling like some far off solar system. As they walked on past the Quokkas, which were grouped playfully at the side of the road, Anne couldn't help remarking how very special the island was.

They made their way down the hill to Thomson Bay and checked into one of the island's restaurants for dinner. The restaurant was busy as usual but they managed to find a table on the terrace overlooking the turquoise ocean and white sandy beach.

'Do you know Kevin I can't think when the last time it was that the three of us were sitting dining at a restaurant together? I mean I know we eat together at home but it's lovely to be actually out in a restaurant once in a while. It's wonderful that we can spend all this time together, we really must do this more often, we have no excuse,' exclaimed Anne as she studied the menu.

'Mum's right, Dad, we must do this more often after all you are the boss, you know. You must start delegating things and it's pointless having all this money and not spending some of it.'

'Now look here you two, I've had enough of this you can stop this nagging right here and now. I've come here for a rest, not to be nagged at, get on with drinking your cocktails and decide what you want from the menu. But I will give you this, you are right we must start spending more time together, it's something that has been on my mind recently after all life is not a rehearsal. Let's just enjoy these few days together and hopefully we can start planning a big holiday together. Here's to a relaxing weekend together and many more of them, yes let's do this more often, cheers,' said Kevin raising his glass.

Kevin McNeil was studying the wine list and just about to order a bottle of his favourite Swan Valley chardonnay when his mobile phone interrupted the proceedings.

'Oh, here we go again, is nowhere safe?' said Anne as she sipped her Singapore sling, 'I thought it wouldn't be long before we would be disturbed with a bloody phone call from work.'

Kevin shook his head and mouthed his apologies to his wife as he got up from the table and took the call in the foyer outside the restaurant.

Minutes later, he returned to the table but he was now as white as a ghost.

'What on earth has happened, you look terrible?' exclaimed Anne anxiously, 'You look to be in a total state of shock, is everything alright, Kevin?'

'I'm afraid not, love, it's work again,' he replied looking at his watch, 'Look, I can't go into any detail here but I have to return to Perth straight away.'

'I don't believe it!' hissed Anne under her breath.

'You stay on the boat and I'll catch the last ferry back which leaves in just under thirty minutes. We have a big problem, Anne, with the latest government order and I must get back there as soon as possible. I'll try and ring you later this evening and explain everything to you. Hopefully, it can be resolved quickly and I can re-join you afterwards probably first thing in the morning. You have everything you need on the boat, of course.'

Kevin blew them both a kiss and dashed out of the restaurant. He made his way quickly down to the quayside where the high speed ferry was waiting and already going through the embarkation process. There was a long queue with several day-trippers waiting to get back on-board for the return journey to B-Shed, Northport and Perth. Kevin took his position at the back of the queue, which moved swiftly, and ten minutes later, he was on-board. He took a seat in the lounge, ordered himself a stiff whisky and sat back.

He had a mix of thoughts and worries racing through his mind. How on earth had pornographic images got onto those devices? Did the new hardware supplier have anything to do with this? Are they even the laptops they have supplied? The phone call he'd received from Ken Diamond had been brief, too brief in fact. All he could tell him was that the Head of Government Services wanted to see them both in his office immediately with regard to the distribution of pornographic material on laptops they had recently delivered. Just over ninety minutes later, after a relatively smooth crossing, he arrived at Elizabeth Quay, Perth. Ken Diamond was waiting patiently for him on the quayside as arranged.

'Ken, what the hell is going on here, have you any ideas what any of this is about?'

'It's a mystery to me, Kevin. I'm sorry to get you back from your trip but all I know is that some of the laptops, not all, I hasten to add, actually contain explicit material. The laptops are from the batch that we recently delivered on that last contract, they are also locked from any possible use apparently. You could say they are as useful as a one armed trapeze artist with an itchy arse.'

'Yes, thanks for that analogy, Ken, this is bloody serious. Have you spoken with anyone else about this?'

'I haven't spoken to anyone in the company, just yourself. I've only spoken to Phil Pleasance who is waiting for us at his office. I told him we are on our way and will get there as soon as we can. Naturally, he is very angry with all this and wants to see us immediately. Come on we need to get a move on before his team leaves the office for the evening.'

They jumped into Ken's Mercedes, which had been parked illegally on Barrack Street just up, from the ferry terminal. The traffic was heavy as they fought their way through the busy rush hour. In fact, it would have been quicker for them to park up somewhere and walk the short distance to the offices on St George's Terrace.

Ten minutes later, they parked illegally again this time on Victoria Avenue. They dashed around the corner and headed for the stairs up to the Government service offices.

As they raced up the stairs and walked through the door, the receptionist was there waiting to escort them into the conference room. There seated before them was Phil Pleasance, Andrew Raynor, Head of Legal Services and a senior police officer. The uniformed officer was clearly high ranking with the insignia of three stars and a crown on his epaulets. Kevin thought he recognised him from possibly one of the weekly television crime reporting programs.

'Come in, gentlemen, and thank you for coming over so swiftly. Before we begin, a few introductions are needed. I think you know Andrew but you possibly haven't met Commander Mick Saunders from Crime Operations.'

Kevin and Ken who were still breathless and both now ashen faced, looked decidedly worried as they each introduced themselves.

Phil Pleasance who was normally a mild and good-natured gentleman opened up the conversation.

'Well, Mr McNeil, I think your sales director has provided you with the basic details but I'll recap just for everyone's benefit. This morning one of our own IT support technicians had the task of installing fifteen laptops in the Police HR department. The laptops were part of a consignment we ordered from your company. On opening the first box and powering the machine up, our technician was about to connect the laptop to the force network and he was horrified to see that pornographic images had replaced the start-up screen. What is more the laptop was frozen and could not be connected to our network.'

'Under the circumstances, this is probably a good thing as we are concerned the laptop operating systems could have infected our own network. Our technician opened nine further boxes with varying results. This is something we are checking now just to be on the safe side. We do not believe all the laptops contain these images but they are all boxed-up at present as part of an ongoing police investigation. We believe the entire order of 100 laptops will have to be thoroughly examined which I am sure you understand is going to be an essential but costly business. We will, of course, be passing the cost of this exercise back to your own company.'

For once, Kevin McNeil was dumbstruck; he tried to respond but he couldn't. He opened his mouth but nothing came out. He stammered his way through some form of a weak apology and eventually he found his voice.

‘Erm, can I firstly please apologise for any distress this has caused. I am sure you will be aware that we knew nothing of this. We only received the shipment ourselves a few days before they were despatched to the government offices and they will have been under lock and key at our warehouse in Fremantle. This looks to me like some form of sabotage. I can assure you at McNeil Industries we operate a strict security…’

At this point, Commander Saunders decided to interrupt Kevin. ‘Mr McNeil, as part of our investigations we will need to examine the security arrangements you have in place and obtain any CCTV footage etc. that you have in operation at the warehouse. It is possible, of course, these pornographic images may have been present on the machines when you received them from the Far East of course, but we will need to look at any CCTV footage whilst they were in storage at your warehouse.’

‘I assume you do have CCTV cameras in the warehouse?’

‘Of course, that won’t be a problem,’ assured Kevin McNeil who was feeling very uncomfortable with the tone of the meeting.

‘And you keep archives of these recordings?’

Kevin McNeil hadn’t a clue on whether they kept recordings or not.

‘Yes, I’m sure we can provide those for you.’

‘You mentioned sabotage, Mr McNeil. Can you think of any reason why someone would do such a thing to these laptops?’ enquired Commander Saunders.

‘No, none at all.’

‘Well, can I ask you something else then?’ continued the commander, ‘Have you had any trouble before with supplies from the Far East?’

‘No, this is the first time; we have been importing goods from there for almost a decade. However, we have just changed supplier and this is clearly worrying that our first delivery has resulted in this incident.’

‘Agreed, it is indeed worrying. Did you not check out the supplier thoroughly before you contracted with them?’

‘Yes, of course I did it myself personally. They seemed to be a reputable quality organisation with a sound track record. We did a due diligence on the company before exchanging contracts,’ responded Kevin as he glanced across at Ken for support, 'I can't think how this could have happened.'

Ken Diamond who was normally never short of something to say for once remained silent.

'Well, gentlemen, unless you have something more to say, I don't think there is much more that we can achieve here and we now need to let the investigation process take its course. You will be hearing from the investigating officers in Crime Operations in the next few days. I have of course instructed our departments that we can no longer receive any further deliveries from your company or for that matter enter into any further contracts with you whilst the investigation takes place. I am sure you understand and thank you for coming across so promptly. Again, thank you for coming over, and I am sure you can find your own way out,' said Phil Pleasance who was clearly rattled by the whole thing and didn't even look up from his notepad.

Kevin McNeil and Ken Diamond bade farewell to the three men seated around the table and made their way sheepishly to the lifts.

'You were strangely bloody quiet in there for once Ken, not a lot of help, I must say!' said Kevin as the lift door closed behind them, 'I'm bloody furious at this lot I can tell you and I won't stop until I find out who it is that is behind this. We have never in the history of the company experienced anything like this. Why on earth didn't you support me in there?'

For one moment, Ken thought about replying that any post sales issues should come under the Operations Director rather than himself, but he thought better of it.

'I couldn't add anything useful, boss. It was a meeting I'd rather not have attended to be quite honest.'

'Well, I bloody would have liked to miss it as well. You can drop me off at home as soon as you can, Ken. I need to start thinking on who it is that is responsible for this because, mark my words, I'll bloody well find out if I have to go to the ends of the earth to do it.'

'What is bothering me at this precise moment, Kevin, is the after effect of all this lot and what it means to the future of the company.'

As they drove off at great speed onto the freeway, neither of them had noticed the parking fine that had been plastered across the car windscreen.

Chapter 10

Friday, 26 February, 2016

HMP Dinas Bay, North Wales

Charlie Ellis had been moved temporarily from his current role on the "A" Wing catering section to support the "D" Wing dining hall, as there was a shortage of kitchen staff following the release of a number of prisoners. He was busy clearing up dishes in the kitchens after lunch when he noticed a familiar face sitting in the far corner of the canteen, someone that he recognised from the past. He simply couldn't take his eyes off him.

At first, he thought it was maybe someone who looked just like him. But no there was no mistake, it was definitely him alright. It was someone who, over the past months, Charlie had grown to dislike intensely. In some ways, he felt Tariq had actually led to his and Tim Ridgway's downfall and subsequent arrest. It was Tariq Atiq who had been involved with them during the fraudulent credit card production. This was the guy who stupidly walked into a bank to withdraw a large sum of money on a stolen card.

So this is where the bugger ended up, thought Charlie. He knew Atiq had been convicted, but he had always assumed he had been sent to a different prison. Without a moment's hesitation, Charlie decided to seek his revenge. There was no love lost between Charlie and Tariq, they had simply never got on, it was almost hate at first sight. He waited for his opportunity at the end of his shift and for all the prisoners to return to their cells from the dining hall. He was just leaving the catering area himself and decided to approach the duty prison officer on the wing.

'Back to your cell, Ellis, your shift is over,' said the prison officer not even bothering to look up from his checklist in front of him.

'Excuse me, sir, but there is something troubling me and I think it is something you need to know.'

'And what would that be, Ellis? No, don't tell me you've decided to poison someone with the custard!' laughed Prison Officer Holbrook dismissively.

'No seriously, sir. I have overheard something earlier. It maybe something or nothing but I felt it should be reported to yourselves.'

'Alright, Ellis, what is it that you've overheard and don't waste my time. What little nugget of information or gem of intelligence do you wish to report?' said the prison officer sarcastically.

'I believe one of the prisoners on this wing, anyway I think his name is Tariq Atiq is offering mobile phones and drugs to other prisoners on "D" wing,' said Charlie in a hushed voice and lying through his teeth. 'My understanding is that he has a stash in his cell apparently and he's been offering it around during lunch. As I say there may be nothing in it, I'm dead against drugs and I felt it my duty to let you know.'

'I see, well thanks for passing it on. I'll report it upstairs. Now in the meantime, Ellis, I suggest you get your arse back to your own wing,' said Officer Holbrook sarcastically, 'I'll escort you there personally just in case you get lost.'

Charlie Ellis returned to his cell with a large grin on his face.

***

Perth, Western Australia

Kevin McNeil had not slept a wink all night, with so much on his mind. He'd paced up and down his bedroom floor in the early hours wondering whether he'd been stitched up by the new hardware suppliers in Singapore or possibly even by one of his own employees, someone perhaps who was disgruntled and jealous of the wealth that McNeil had accumulated over the years. Sure, the laptops had been a bargain but they were after all high quality machines and the promise of future large orders had led to McNeil receiving a huge discount on this first batch from his new suppliers. He'd decided that his first priority however had to be returning to Rottnest Island. After all, he'd abandoned his wife Anne and step daughter Karen on their yacht there. So rising early, he took a taxi down to the Elizabeth Quay at Perth and caught the first High Speed ferry from Pier 2 over to Rottnest. His own internal investigations into the laptop incident would just have to wait for now. He now had some explaining to do to Anne and Karen on his untimely departure from the island.

***

It hadn't taken long for news to filter out regarding the problem laptops being delivered to Police HQ despite the HR department trying to keep the lid on the whole sorry saga. Soon the rumour mill was churning out all sorts of different variations of the story and the press was starting to have a field day. One completely untrue rumour circulating was that the Police network itself had been hacked into. It was even suggested it was now riddled with pornographic material that was now finding its way onto other systems including the neighbourhood watch system.

Lance Smithson was the first to hear about it in Gforce following a phone call from one of his government clients. Lance couldn't believe his ears and decided that whilst it didn't warrant a full board meeting, he should call an urgent management meeting at short notice to discuss what it could mean for the future of their own company.

The senior management team as requested assembled in the small conference room and Lance relayed to them what he had just heard.

'Gentlemen, you will now have heard that an investigation is taking place with regard to that recent government order of laptops from McNeil Industries. You will also recall that despite our heavily discounted proposal McNeil once again won the business. As it has turned out, gentlemen, perhaps on this occasion we have had a good miss with this contract and I think we can look forward to an interesting few months ahead! However, following this last government tender it is clear to me that we have a mole in our camp and this is something I plan to unearth.'

The room was now filled with laughter.

***

Handforth Dean, Cheshire

Alan Ravenscroft and his wife Helen were out doing their weekly shop at the nearest large supermarket. Alan didn't normally accompany his wife on the weekly shopping trip. But on this occasion, he needed to combine the trip to a nearby department store with him trying on a new suit for a forthcoming wedding that they had just been invited to. They were waiting patiently in the queue at the supermarket checkout when Alan noticed someone familiar. Someone he hadn't seen for quite some time who had just paid for his goods and was about to leave the store.

'I'm sorry about this, love, but I won't be a minute, there is someone I haven't seen for a long while and I need to speak with him urgently,' said Alan as he dashed off towards the store exit.

The store was always very busy on the Friday evening and when Alan eventually fought his way through the crowds of shoppers and finally reached the huge car park there was no sign at all of the man.

Alan made his way back to the checkout till where his wife was now settling the bill.

'Did you find whoever it was that you were in a hurry to see, love?' enquired Helen Ravenscroft as she handed her credit card to the assistant.

'No, I think I might have been mistaken,' replied Alan breathlessly as he loaded the six bottles of red wine into the canvas bottle carrier.

'So, who did you think it was anyway?'

'I thought it was someone who used to work for us. Do you remember Paul Arrowsmith? He was one of our programmers a few years back.'

‘Yes, I remember him. He was a very nice lad, quiet, shy sort of person I seem to remember.’

‘Yes, that’s him. Well, I don’t think it could have been him anyway, as he is in Australia as far as I know. Still, it certainly looked just like him; it was the spitting image. He could have been his identical twin brother.’

***

At precisely 10:15 am, the Rottnest express ferry docked at Thomson Bay and Kevin McNeil was the first passenger to disembark; he made his way up the hill to Porpoise Bay just in time for a late breakfast on the yacht. As he approached the boat, he could see Anne and Karen enjoying their breakfast in the early morning sun.

‘Oh, so you’ve decided to join us after all, Kevin. That’s nice that you could spare the time to come over after abandoning both of us yesterday in that restaurant. We had to walk back to the boat on our own in the dark. And now I suppose you want some breakfast, well you know where the galley is,’ shouted Anne McNeil as Kevin climbed on board.

‘Please don’t start, Anne. You know I’ve got a lot on my plate at present. I was left with no option but to get over there and it’s still not sorted. I can’t ever see it being sorted to be honest.’

‘But you could have dealt with it on the phone surely, Kevin, it could be sorted out by other people in the company. You are the boss, for god’s sake, why do you pay all these people these high salaries working for you, wouldn’t it have waited till Tuesday?’

‘No chance of that, I’m afraid, love, I did see a different side to Phil Pleasance yesterday. He insisted on seeing both Ken and I face to face that evening. You don’t seem to realise the trouble the company is in and the repercussions that could follow from this.’

‘I don’t care what trouble the company is in. I’m sick of the bloody company, that’s all we hear about. You should be relaxing now, not working every hour god sends.’

Kevin was now losing his patience and the tone had changed somewhat.

‘Oh, but you like the money that the company brings in,’ snapped Kevin, ‘Not to mention the dividends you get each year, don’t forget about that. You wouldn’t be able to enjoy your lifestyle without the success of the business that I’ve worked so hard for.’

‘Hang on, I’ve been behind you all the way, supporting you, don’t forget that.’

‘Will you two please stop arguing, you are like two little children,’ interjected Karen who was now wishing she had stayed behind at home.

‘Yes, you are right, Karen. Let’s just enjoy the rest of the weekend if we possibly can, we’ll say no more about it,’ replied Kevin as he opened a carton of orange juice and wishing it was something a bit stronger.

But try as he might, Kevin couldn’t get the laptop incident out of his mind. It was gnawing away at him like a dog gnawing a bone; it was like a festering sore. In all the years he’d been trading, he’d never experienced anything like this. Suddenly, he found his entrepreneurial spirit dwindling rapidly.

Chapter 11

Sunday, 28 February, 2016

All through the weekend, Kevin McNeil had constantly been moaning about the situation that the company had now found itself in with the government. Instead of this being a time for relaxation for the whole family, it had turned out to be a complete disaster. There was no way they would be having the enjoyable weekend they had promised themselves. It had got to the point that Kevin's wife Anne had therefore instructed him in no uncertain terms to turn the boat around and head back home, quite simply she'd had enough. She wasn't interested in the detail. They had arrived back at the Perth Royal Yacht Club marina on the Sunday afternoon a day ahead of when they first planned to return.

Kevin was still in shock with what had happened and he was quieter than normal. All the way home in the car you could hear a pin drop with the silence. When they eventually arrived home at The Vines, he quickly got changed and headed into his study to catch up on the hundreds of emails he'd been receiving since news of the incident had started to leak out. The most disturbing email he'd received was the one from his new hardware supplier in Singapore. They had made it quite clear, in no uncertain terms, that they were now terminating their contract with McNeil Industries and that they would be looking now for new distribution channels in Australia. He was amazed that they had even heard about it unless someone had deliberately informed them.

As he ploughed through the emails, he was also disturbed to have a large number from his current employees who somehow had heard about the incident. They were all concerned about their jobs and the future of the company. He decided after pouring himself a stiff whisky that he must write an open letter to all employees and try to at least stabilise the situation within the company. An hour later, he'd finished compiling the letter explaining the situation and reassuring them that the company still had a large order book and a strong future ahead of it. He then emailed the letter to his PA Jane Paterson requesting that the letter should be distributed across all the company employees first thing on the Monday morning.

***

It had been on Alan Ravenscroft's mind since Friday, he was so convinced he'd seen Paul Arrowsmith at the local supermarket. He'd not settled all weekend and he'd gone through a number of possibilities, had Paul Arrowsmith decided that Australia wasn't for him after all and decided to return home or was he simply returning home to see his family? Either way it was very odd. It was only last month he'd received the call from Richard Ashcroft requesting a reference and the company had clearly indicated that he was enjoying his new life down under. He thought about calling the company in Australia but had lost their contact details, which he'd scribbled on a notepad. He'd remembered the name Richard Ashcroft but hadn't made a note of the company name. He'd been in such a rush to go to lunch that day. Try as he might, he couldn't get it out of his mind and he decided to call an old friend who worked at the Midshire Police Computer Department.

'I'm just going to make a phone call, love,' he said as he left the lounge and headed into his study. He picked up the phone and dialled the number from memory.

'George? It's a long time no speak, it's Alan Ravenscroft here. I trust you and Chrissy are well?'

'Hi, Alan, yes it's good to hear from you. We are both well, thanks. Guess what? I finally retired from Midshire Police a couple of weeks back and the missus has found me a list of jobs around the house but at least I get a lie in now in the mornings,' laughed George, 'Anyway, how can I help you?'

'Well George, this is maybe something or nothing but when you were at Midshire Police did you work alongside Paul Arrowsmith in the computer department?'

'I certainly did. Paul was a grand lad, a bit shy but a cracking programmer worth his weight in gold. Hang on, didn't he work for you at one time? A great guy, why do you ask, what's he done?'

'Oh, it's nothing really, but has he recently emigrated to Australia?'

'No, has he buggery. What on earth made you think that? He came to my leaving do only last week. He's still at Midshire Police, he was telling me on the night that he's just had a big promotion apparently and is very settled there from what I can gather.'

Alan was suddenly lost for words.

'Alan, are you still there? The line seems to have gone dead. Hello, Alan!'

'Yes, I'm sorry George, I was just thinking to myself. Well, do you know whether he has recently returned from Australia perhaps from a short holiday or visiting friends?' said Alan who was just trying to think straight for a moment.

'No, not as far as I'm aware Alan. In fact, Australia would probably be the last place you'd find him. I think he has a fear of flying. I don't think he's taken any holidays for quite a while. He's a bit of a workaholic you know.'

'Yes, I remember he was a hard worker, a top bloke.'

'Is there anything wrong, Alan? I can probably get hold of his phone number if you want it. I'm sure he'd be pleased to hear from you.'

'No, it's fine George. Look we must get together now you've retired and you have plenty of time on your hands. I'll be in touch soon. Bye for now, best wishes to Chrissy.'

Alan replaced the receiver and thought for a moment on what should be his next move. Was he interfering into something out of his control? After five minutes in deep thought, he then grabbed his coat from the hallway and returned to the living room where his wife was watching the TV.

‘I’m just popping out for a minute, Helen, I shouldn’t be too long.’

Alan made his way down the avenue and took the short walk across the park to the town centre. The snowdrops and crocuses in the park looked delightful and were now heralding the start of spring. He still hesitated as to whether he was doing the right thing but decided to go ahead anyway and climbed the three stone steps up to the entrance of the old police station building. He pushed open the large creaking oak door. It was like going back in time, Alan thought surely this particular police station must be one of the oldest in the country and should be on the list for replacement. It would have made a good police museum and if Dixon of Dock Green had stepped out of the building, he wouldn’t have looked out of place. The oak front desk was empty with no one in sight, it was early Sunday evening, mild for the time of year and everywhere was quiet. The neighbourhood watch and cybercrime awareness posters around the wall were the only clues that this was in fact the 21st century. The polished mahogany desk was bare with just a large old fashioned brass bell on display. He rang the desk bell and sat down on the hard bench opposite and waited. Minutes later, a young fresh faced police constable arrived from a side office behind the desk.

Alan thought it is true what they say, they do seem to look younger every day.

‘I’m sorry about the wait, sir. I was just on the phone to someone. Now how can I help you?’

‘Well officer, my name is Alan Ravenscroft and I am not sure but I think I may have spotted some sort of identity theft that I think you should be aware of.’

The police officer looked puzzled, ‘Really and how is that, sir?’

Alan related the phone call that he had first received requesting a reference and then a few weeks later his sighting locally of Paul Arrowsmith himself. To Alan’s disappointment, the officer didn’t seem at all interested in his story neither did he look convinced that anything was amiss. In short, he didn’t really know what to with the information that Alan was providing.

‘Well I suppose he could have returned to the UK in that time,’ volunteered the young police officer who was clearly not convinced at Alan’s story.

'I don't think so officer as I checked with an old friend who worked with him, he doesn't believe he actually went to Australia in the first place. As a matter of fact, officer, the potential victim I am referring to still works here at Midshire Police. Paul Arrowsmith is a computer programmer in your own computer department. Perhaps you should call him when he's next in tomorrow morning to alert him that someone may be possibly using his identity.'

'Well I shall take down the details, sir, and will do exactly that.'

The police officer continued to note down all the details including Alan's name, address and contact phone number.

'Well, sir, I think I have everything I need here, thanks for coming in and rest assured I'll follow this up for you.'

Alan made his way back home and he thought short of ringing Paul Arrowsmith himself there was nothing more that he could do. The police officer returned to the back office and filed the note in his in-tray. Unfortunately, he was off duty later that night and then on leave for two weeks.

***

Monday, 29 February, 2016

Kevin McNeil was the first to arrive and opened up the office on the Monday morning at 7am. When Jane Paterson, his PA arrived just after 8am, he was already hard at work studying the forecast reports that had been produced long before the unfortunate events of the previous week.

'Good morning, Kevin. I didn't expect to see you in the office until tomorrow for the sales meeting. Did you have a good weekend, you went sailing didn't you?'

'Good morning, Jane. Yes, we went sailing alright, but I'm sorry to tell you that the company has now entered very stormy waters if you can forgive the pun! I'm afraid I had to cut short the long weekend away after all that saga with the government laptops. With a likely reduction in government business, I'm just working on the forecast to see how it affects the months ahead.

I'll probably take this lot home with me and work on it there without the phone interruptions.'

'Sorry, what do you mean the saga with the government laptops?'

Jane looked confused and it became immediately apparent to Kevin that somehow she didn't know anything whatsoever about the laptop incident from the previous week.

'I think you'd better sit down, Jane. It is not good news at all I'm afraid. I sent you an email yesterday afternoon which you probably haven't had time to read yet. I'm afraid our company is heading for what you could call a very bumpy ride and the sooner we get to grips with it the better.'

Kevin then explained the full situation to her and tried to put some sort of a positive spin on it all particularly on how he planned to try at least to limit the damage. But deep down he knew it did not look good for the future of the company at this point in time.

'So are we going to issue some sort of press statement? I mean we can't simply sit back and let bad news leak out like this, it's far too damaging,' said Jane taking a seat at the side of his desk.

'Well naturally, we will do everything we can Jane but to be honest there is not much we can do at present, the police are investigating the whole damn situation. In the meantime, can you please circulate the email that I sent to you yesterday for all employees and shareholders? Our starting point must be to keep them in the loop. I am going to work on these forecasts back at home and will call you later. You can reach me there if you need me.'

Kevin placed the forecast reports in his briefcase and was just about to get back in the car to head home when his mobile rang. It was Peter Osbourne, the Head of Information Technology.

'G'day, Peter and how are you?'

'I'm glad I've caught you, Kevin. Jane said that you had been in the office.'

'It's good to hear from you, Peter. I trust everything is at least going well with the new online sales website?'

'I'm afraid not, Kevin and that's why I'm ringing you. I have some bad news. We've been hacked over the weekend, the new online retail site has been hit with a Trojan of some kind. It's ransomware and they are demanding payment to decrypt our data! We have had to take the system down immediately. It has also infected our order book.'

'The online order book?' gasped Kevin who didn't think he could take much more bad news.

'No, it's both I'm afraid, online and the live database. I'm afraid our master customer database has also been corrupted. Whoever did this knew exactly what they were doing, we've been targeted well and truly and I'm sorry to bring you this news, Kevin, but we thought you needed to know as soon as possible!'

'Any idea on how this actually attacked us, Peter?'

'Yes, we believe someone emailed us with a phishing attempt with some sort of special offer. It only needed one of our staff to respond to allow the malware in. It was probably something like an offer of a free holiday on social media or something along those lines.'

'What! And when do you expect it will be fixed?'

'I can't say at present, Kevin, but our guys are working on it to firstly remove the offending code before we start restoring any of the data. The buggers are even demanding a ransom of $10,000 to release the encryption but we are not giving into them as we have backups. My best guess would be that we should be up and running on Wednesday at the earliest.'

'Oh god, that's all I need.'

***

Chapter 12

Tuesday, 1 March, 2016

Hywel Jones, one of the security officers at HMP Dinas Bay, was manning the security office on his own. He was wading through the backlog of incident reports and deciding which ones could be just filed or needed some form of follow up. They were badly short of staff and way behind in assessing the intelligence reports through the lack of resources. He was part way through reading the report from the weekend from Officer Keith Holbrook regarding the information provided by inmate Charlie Ellis when his boss Tom Fletcher came bursting into the office.

'Good morning, Hywel and a Happy St David's day to you. Nice to see you wearing the daffodil this morning. Look sorry about this, but I need a big favour from you.'

'Bore Da, good morning, sir. Yes of course, how can I help?' replied Hywel as he closed the intelligence report.

'Well, I'm sorry to have to ask you this, Hywel, as, I appreciate, you really are snowed under a bit at present. But is there any chance you can help out on "B" wing this morning. They are also a bit short staffed and they could do with another pair of hands down there? It's only for today of course. I'll get someone to cover for you here.'

'Yes, no problem, sir. I'll get down there straight away,' responded Hywel as he filed the intelligence report under no further action, relieved to get away from the growing pile of paperwork.

***

Perth, Western Australia

The pilot scheme of the first components of the Project Watchman module had been brought forward and was scheduled to start today. Software development of the additional code had gone very well. It was now well ahead of its original schedule. So it was decided to push on with the other development phases, and run a trial on just the vehicle and face recognition aspects. The development team had released two prototype programs to the speed camera supplier, who had followed instructions and embedded the software routines in a number of cameras. These cameras would then replace the ones at a number of fixed locations throughout the Perth and Fremantle districts.

It had been decided in the early stages of the project that the exact pilot locations would be kept secret even from the software development team. The trial which consisted of monitoring speed cameras and limited facial recognition analysis would be implemented initially at the closely guarded secret locations. Data from the trial sites would be automatically transmitted back to the Watchman server at Police HQ. Only two people knew of the exact locations of these cameras and that was the Project Director and the camera support technician himself. Both were sworn to secrecy not to release any information on their whereabouts.

***

'Have you seen their share price lately?' shouted Jim Walker across to Lance Smithson as he entered the open plan office area.

'Go on, make my day, Jim!' replied Lance carrying his mug of coffee and stopping short of entering his own office.

'It's now down from $3.50 to $1.20.'

'Has it indeed!' replied Lance with a huge smile on his face.

'Can you believe it, Lance, on how fast word has got around that they are in serious trouble. In my opinion, it serves them bloody right nicking business unethically.'

'Well to be honest, Jim, it's only the government contracts that are affecting them at present. They are still very strong in some of the other sectors. We daren't take our eye off the ball with them. McNeil is a devious little bugger and he's probably already worked out his recovery plan. But I haven't quite finished with him just yet, you wait and see,' said Lance tapping the side of his nose.

Chapter 13

Friday, 4 March, 2016

John Edmonds had decided to take a week off. He had treated his wife to a cheap package holiday to Bali to celebrate their wedding anniversary. Since leaving McNeil Industries and joining Gforce Technologies, he'd had no time off. Apart from the odd long weekend, he hadn't had a single break. His wife Sandra, who worked part time at the local bakery shop, insisted that they desperately needed some time away together.

John and Sandra Edmonds had been married for four years and lived in Canning Vale, a southern suburb about 20km from the Perth city centre. They lived with Sandra's mother Mary. It was not an ideal setup with Mary constantly arguing with both her daughter and son-in-law. At times, the atmosphere in the house was unbearable. John was working all the hours he could to raise enough money for a deposit to buy their own house but for the time being they just had to make do and get on with it.

They drove over to Perth International Airport and he parked the car in the long stay car park. They wheeled their cases across to the terminal building and joined the lengthy queue for the check in desks.

'I'm really looking forward to getting on that beach and chilling out, I can't wait,' exclaimed Sandra.

'Well, at least we are away from your mother for the next week, love!' said John as they moved gradually with their trolley in the queue.

'Yes, you can say that again. No more bickering or nagging. I can't tell you how much I really need this holiday but I can't think what you are doing bringing your blooming laptop, John. I hope you are not planning to work whilst we are away. I'm looking forward to this holiday and I don't want to see you with your head stuck in that bloody thing when we should be relaxing on the beach.'

'I've only brought it to keep in touch with friends on email. I promise I won't be going anywhere near the work documents as they are on my other laptop back in the office.'

'Good and that's where they had better stay,' replied the domineering Sandra Edmonds as they waited for their turn to check in for the four hour flight.

The airport was busy as usual but the check-in queue moved rapidly and twenty minutes later they had checked in for the Air Asia flight to Denpasar. They followed the other passengers into the security check area and took their place in the long queue. After moving through the body scanners, they collected their belongings from the conveyor belt and proceeded to replace their belts and shoes. They hadn't, at that time, noticed one of the security officers nodding across to his colleague. As they were about to continue onwards into the departure lounge, they were approached by a security officer.

'Excuse me, sir, but can you please step into the office? We just need to ask you a few questions.'

'Yes, what seems to be the trouble? I passed everything through the scanner,' responded John Edmonds nervously.

'As I say we just need to ask you a few questions, sir. It shouldn't take too long, can you please step this way,' repeated the officer.

'I'm afraid we don't have time for this officer, we have a plane to catch and we don't have much time, so can we please be on our way. If this is a random search, can you please choose someone else as we are in a hurry,' interjected Sandra Edmonds somewhat arrogantly, as she attempted to usher her husband out of the security area.

'I don't think so, madam. I'm afraid the two of you will have to come this way. Now, if you could please step into the office.'

'But this is ridiculous, what is it that we have supposed to have done?' cried Sandra Edmonds, who by now was deliberately creating a scene and drawing attention from the other passengers.

The officer didn't respond and politely escorted John and Sandra Edmonds into the adjacent office closing the door behind them.

John Edmonds was about to ask him again on what the problem was and why they were being retained, but Sandra stepped in and beat him to it.

'I shall ask you again, officer, what is it that we have supposed to have done?'

'All in good time, madam. Now can you both please sit down? Can you place the laptop bag on the desk, sir?' replied the officer who was now snapping on a pair of blue protective gloves.

John Edmonds placed the bag on the table and the officer proceeded to rifle through the contents of the bag. Five minutes later, having found nothing of any real interest, the officer handed the bag towards John Edmonds.

'OK, can you please remove your laptop from the bag, Mr Edmonds, and place it on the desk.'

'But it's already been through the scanner officer,' said John now starting to protest.

'I realise that, Mr Edmunds. Please place it on the desk,' responded the officer.

John at first thought how is it that he knows my name but maybe he saw the boarding card in the tray on the conveyor belt. He thought no more of it and did what he was told removing the laptop from the bag and placing it in front of the officer.

'Can you please switch it on and enter the login details please, sir?'

'Yes, of course. What's this all about officer, it's my home use laptop.'

The officer remained silent, nodded and indicated for John to enter the details at the login prompt.

John did exactly what he was told. He entered the password and handed the laptop to the officer who proceeded to explore the files on the hard drive. It was as if he knew exactly where to look.

'Right, so you say this is your home use laptop, sir?'

'That's right, I just brought it on holiday to keep in touch on email and social media, you know that sort of thing. My business laptop is back in the office.'

‘Well, sir, we have reason to believe that you have obtained a number of confidential documents that do not belong to yourself and that you are maybe considering passing these onto another organisation.’

‘That’s ridiculous officer. This is my personal use laptop, why would I have documents belonging to someone else?’

‘So perhaps you can explain how you come to have a large number of folders and files belonging to a company called Gforce Technologies?’

‘I haven’t and in any case that’s who I work for!’

‘Well I wonder how these have got in here then,’ the officer responded pointing to the files,’ as you can see, sir, they are all marked Government Secure & Company Confidential – Directors’ eyes only. You are not a director, are you? I assume you do actually work for Gforce and you don’t work for the government?’

John was shocked. He couldn’t remember moving or copying any business files onto his personal use laptop. True, he knew he’d been taking a risk a few weeks ago when he had been passing the odd sales pricing document to McNeil Industries for a few extra dollars, but he had no intention of passing on these types of documents. He didn’t even know that he had access to them.

For once Sandra Edmonds was quieter than normal, not even a whimpered protest.

‘Yes, I’ve told you I work for Gforce and no I’m not a director. Look I have no idea how those files have got there, someone must have planted them there. I’ve never even seen them before.’

‘Well I think you’ll need to tell that to the authorities, sir. In the meantime, you are under arrest.’

***

Kevin McNeil had decided to call an urgent board meeting for the Friday morning. He felt he had no option but to share his concerns with all board directors. The five men and two women had assembled in the board room early to hear how Kevin’s plans would hopefully start turning the failing business around. They had expected to hear a positive spin on things but were in for a shock when Kevin addressed them.

'Thank you all for coming over. Look I'll keep it brief as I am sure you have already seen the latest share price of the company which is now trading at just seventy-five cents per share and plummeting fast. It has never been that low in the company's existence and the recent bad publicity is pushing it down even lower. I feel now is the time that looking at the downturn of the order book, we will have no option but to start closing parts of the business down or at the very least placing some of the employees on short time working.'

'But is there nothing we can do, Kevin. I mean surely our other non-government sales orders are still coming through as normal?' exclaimed Paul Turner the Operations Director who hadn't realised the situation was quite as bad as it was.

'No, I'm afraid not, Paul. They have also dried up, bad news has travelled fast, too fast. I'm sorry to have to tell you. We always said Perth has a very active grapevine and this just proves it. Ken can give you the full sales picture for the next six months in a moment. We have already had to close the Brisbane and Sydney offices. The planned new development of warehouse facilities in Fremantle has also been cancelled.'

'I can't tell you how much this hurts me having built up the business from nothing. I am hoping we can at least retain the Western Australia operations to support some of the existing retail branches. As from next Monday, we have no option and we are having to let go almost three hundred of our hard working employees. This, I assure you, breaks my heart but we really have no choice if we are to remain in business. I have asked HR to prepare redundancy lists based on years of service and job roles.'

'Is there no alternative to this, Kevin, couldn't we perhaps team up with Gforce Technologies who at least seemed to be on a roll?'

Kevin looked as though he was going to explode.

'Over my dead body, Ken. There is no way that I'll team up with that lot. They are on a roll because they are winning OUR business. No, we have to try and ride this out, the market will change soon,' replied Kevin who knew that deep down it was just a matter of time before he also had to start laying off the very same directors and senior management seated in front of him around the table.

***

Chapter 14

Monday, 7 March, 2016

A Gforce Technologies employee has been arrested at Perth International Airport over the weekend following a data breach which may have exposed competitive and confidential information belonging to several business customers including Government papers.

The unnamed 28-year-old male was arrested on Tuesday at the Airport prior to boarding an aircraft bound for Bali. He is being held in custody in connection with a recent fraud investigation.

The company has not yet disclosed whether data belonging to several business customers has been leaked, sold, or passed onto competitive companies. It is not yet known what actual data has been stolen but it is believed to consist of names, addresses, and financial data.

Gforce Technologies has notified customers whose data is believed to be involved in the data leak. The arrested employee who is also believed to be working for McNeil Industries is still being held at Perth Central Police station. A spokesman from McNeil Industries was unavailable for comment.

***

Paul Arrowsmith arrived into the office on the Monday morning very early. He had tried everything he could to try and determine the location of the Project Watchman speed cameras which had been modified for the trial. He had started befriending the Project Director even going as far as drinking with him after work. But the whole thing was being kept as a closely guarded secret. Despite several grovelling attempts and getting to the point in showing far too much interest, he eventually decided to resort to seeing if he could get access to the files that were held in the Project Directors office. He took the lift to the fifth floor and made his way through to the open plan office area. The office was deserted; most of the staff would have still been in bed or at home having breakfast.

He tried the door to the Director's office, unsurprisingly, it was locked but he had noticed on previous occasions that the project secretary kept a key in her drawer for emergencies. He opened the drawer and found a bunch of keys, after fumbling and trying different ones out for about five minutes, he eventually managed to open the door. It was still very early and the project team was not expected in for about an hour. There on the desk was a black leather folder marked '**Watchman**' in gold letters, he carefully opened the folder and started to browse carefully through the paperwork. There he found what he was looking for; an A4 envelope marked "*Camera Locations*".

The envelope was fortunately not sealed, he took out the three-page document inside and glanced down the list of some fifty locations but he was in for a shock. The locations had all been coded. They meant nothing to him and instead of showing a street address or a postcode; they each contained a scrambled code word of some description. He thought about photocopying it, but just then heard the lift door closing shut. He hurriedly placed everything back where it came from, locked the office door, returned the bunch of keys and had just had time to sit down at his desk when in walked the Project Director Adam Taylor.

'G'day, Paul, you are bright and early this morning, couldn't you sleep?'

'Good morning, Adam, something like that. I had a few issues on my mind and needed to try a couple of things out,' replied Paul who was now pretending to study a technical specification on his desk.

'So how is that work on the new module coming along?' enquired Adam as he unlocked his office door.

‘Well I’ve only just started on it, Adam. I think it will be quite something once this is in operation.’

Paul had now been tasked with developing what was known as the Time Detection module. This highly innovative and unique piece of software had been designed to be used by any investigating police or fire officer and would be the cornerstone of Project Watchman. It would be the first port of call after an incident to determine what had been going on just prior to and immediately after any incident. Everything in a single report would be available to the officer, video footage, vehicle movements, facial recognition suggestions, persons of interest at the scene, sat nav data etc.

‘I’m looking forward to seeing the first prototype, Paul, keep up the good work. We do seem to be ahead of schedule at present which is great news. I can tell you now, Phil Pleasance is delighted with the progress we are making,’ replied Adam as he closed the office door behind him.

***

Life in the McNeil household had taken a significant turn for the worse. Kevin had been under huge pressure and it had affected his home life. Relationships were not going well and Kevin and Anne were constantly at each other’s throats. The situation had now got to the point that daughter Karen had already decided that she could no longer stand the constant rowing between her stepfather Kevin and her mum Anne. So she had moved out over the weekend to stay with her close friend Jane at nearby Guildford. Kevin was working all the hours he could now to try and keep his business afloat. But try as he might, the company was going downhill fast. The business was losing so much money every day with closures of most of the retail shops. Kevin was also now forced to sell off some of the properties that he had invested in to pay for the redundancy payments and salaries/wages of the remaining staff.

He arrived home from work exhausted on this particular evening to find that the Range Rover was no longer parked in the driveway. He opened the garage door but there was no sign of the vehicle. He’d rung several times earlier to say that he was on his way home but there had been no reply. He made his way into the kitchen and there on the granite worktop was a handwritten note from his wife.

Tuesday 8th March 2016
Dear Kevin

For some time now I've felt that our marriage was no longer working and I'm simply not prepared to put up with the constant rowing we have over the business. Believe me, I have tried to make this marriage work and I've given this a lot of thought but after much consideration, I have decided to leave you, I think it is in both our interests.

I've felt like this for a long time and I think it's for the best. The recent business problem that the company has encountered was the last straw. This is not just over the past few weeks which I know have been hard for you but we've grown apart over the past year I'm afraid. We have had some good times, you and I with some nice memories but the business always seemed to take first place. I am however so grateful that you have also been the father figure that Karen so badly needed.

I have been in touch with Karen and she is joining me.

Please don't try and find us as I think it's time for us both to go our own separate ways and start a new life.

I enjoyed it while it lasted and I wish you well.
Anne

Kevin collapsed and slumped himself down in an armchair. He had been so busy with his own company problems that he hadn't seen it coming at all. How had it come to this, he thought and all in such a short time? The year 2016 was turning out to be a disastrous year for McNeil but he was determined to try and get back to some normality. He was completely stressed out, exhausted and on the verge of a nervous breakdown. He wondered how much longer he could cope with it all. He reached out for the whisky bottle and was just about to pour himself a stiff drink when the phone rang. He dashed across to pick it up hoping it was Anne, maybe she had changed her mind and was on her way back home. He simply couldn't see how he could survive without her.

'Hello, is that Kevin McNeil?' asked the voice on the other end.

'Yes it is, who is it calling?'

'This is Graham Evans from the WA Courier here. We are following up on a reported news item regarding your company and would be interested to hear your side of it before we go into publication.'

'And what news article would that be?'

'Well, we understand that one of your ex-employees has been selling company confidential documents back to you from a rival company. Is this correct, have you anything to say?'

Kevin slammed the phone down hard.

***

Chapter 15

Tuesday, 15 March, 2016

The HMP Dinas Bay Operations team were in the middle of conducting their monthly review with each of the wings in the prison. A senior duty officer from each wing plus the HMP Security team attended the meeting chaired by the Head of Security. The purpose of the meeting was to discuss any problem issues and potential threats that had been previously identified against their relevant wing. It was an initiative that was instigated by the new prison governor as a quality check to ensure that nothing had been missed from previous intelligence reports. All too often in the past information had been overlooked resulting in situations which could have been avoided. The chairman was in the process of reviewing "D" wing activity.

'Gentlemen, we have a disturbing and emerging issue that has been identified, which needs immediate attention before it gets out of control. There are two major problems that have been identified with "D" wing according to the monthly reports and these are as follows. Firstly, drugs, which as you know is now becoming a huge problem throughout the prison in any case. Secondly, and in particular on this wing grooming for terrorism. We need to identify who the offenders are here before it gets out of hand.'

'I think it already has, sir, and what is more, we don't seem to be doing anything about it,' said Officer Holbrook who had been quiet up until this moment. For quite a while, he had been disillusioned with the way the prison security team had been dealing with the intelligence reports that had been previously submitted.

'And what makes you say that, Officer Holbrook?' responded Tom Fletcher who was now looking somewhat uneasy and was suddenly not happy to be on the back foot.

'Well sir, for example, I'm really surprised that nothing was done about the intelligence report that I myself submitted a couple of weeks ago. It may have been something or nothing but the intelligence I had gained certainly mentioned an individual on "D" wing. As far as I can tell the intelligence report seems to have been ignored. Information relating to an inmate who it is believed to be pushing drugs yet as far as I can see it wasn't even pursued.'

'Did you include all the relevant information, Officer Holbrook, names, dates etc. that sort of thing?'

'Yes, most certainly, sir. I included all that information on the inmate who is believed to be also selling mobile phones and pushing drugs on the wing. '

'And which cell and who is it exactly we are talking about?'

Officer Holbrook leafed through his notepad just to confirm the name and quickly found the record.

'A prisoner in cell number D73 known as Tariq Atiq, sir.'

'Is this right, Hywel? Do you have any recollection of this particular intelligence report?'

'Well, vaguely sir. We do get a great number of intelligence reports to assess these days and we can't possibly follow up each one. We do have to prioritise these as much as possible. I'm sure you understand how busy we have all been, sir,' replied Hywel desperately struggling with an excuse.

'And did we not take any action on this?'

'Apparently not, sir. It looks like this one has somehow got through the net.'

Tom Fletcher who was normally very placid looked as though he was about to explode.

'Well, it's time we damn well did do something about it. The net as you call it seems to have bloody large holes in it as far as I can see!' replied Tom Fletcher who was now thumping the table, 'What is the point of intelligence being reported by our officers and logged into the prison security database if we don't take any action on them? We are not filing this stuff for the bloody sake of it, you know. Now make sure we add this one onto Sunday's action list, this wants following up pronto.'

'Yes, sir,' replied Hywel who was now looking very embarrassed and already frantically scribbling in his notebook.

***

'Kevin, there are two police officers outside who wish to see you urgently. Shall I ask them to go through to the conference room or shall I send them into your office?' asked Jane Paterson on the intercom.

'Oh right, thanks Jane. Yes, please show them into the conference room and tell them I'll be across there in a moment.'

Kevin McNeil put on his suit jacket and sat there for a moment collecting his thoughts. He hadn't heard from the police until now and he had been wondering on how the laptop investigation was progressing. Maybe at last they had discovered how the laptops had been corrupted and they could get on with business again or was he about to get a grilling on the source of his supplies. He made his way across the corridor into the large conference room. As he entered the room, the two detectives who were now huddled in quiet conversation stopped and stood up acknowledging his arrival.

'Good morning, sir, we won't keep you long. My name is Inspector Randall and this is my colleague Sergeant Brown. We have been investigating the incident involving your company delivering laptops as part of a recent government order. The laptops as you will recall contained pornographic material. It's been a couple of weeks now since the incident and we felt we needed to update you of our progress to date.'

'Thank you, inspector. Yes, it had gone a bit quiet. I thought with the amount of time spent on this you would have solved this by now,' said Kevin McNeil somewhat arrogantly, 'I had been wondering how this was progressing. I trust that my staff members have been helpful towards your investigation?'

'Yes, they have been most helpful, Mr McNeil. However, we have interviewed your night watchman at great length and he hasn't been able to tell us anything. In fact, he was surprised to hear about the whole affair. He hadn't even heard about the laptop incident which we find quite odd. Clearly, there is some sort of communication problem there. Anyway, that aside, we are satisfied having spoken also to your hardware supplier that the equipment arrived here from Singapore satisfactorily, but we believe someone shortly afterwards broke into your warehouse and sabotaged the laptops. Unfortunately, your CCTV cameras are not…erm…how shall I put it and not to put too fine a point on it, pretty much worthless. You may as well have dummy cameras up there. They are either so badly positioned or not working at all and we strongly recommend that you rectify these as soon as possible. We can always bring in our crime prevention guys if you need advice on where to put these.'

Sergeant Brown thought to himself, *I know where I'd like to put them.*

Both police officers had earlier discussed in the car on the way over how ironic this situation was that a company who specialised in the supply of computers, electronics and camera surveillance equipment did not even have a satisfactory CCTV system operating themselves in their own warehouse. The inspector had remarked to the sergeant it was like the old adage of "*cobblers children who had nothing to wear on their feet*".

'We, therefore, haven't been able to get any video evidence from these which I'm sure you agree would have been most helpful under the circumstances,' continued the inspector. 'However, on examination of the car park perimeter fence, we have discovered that it has been recently cut and this is where we believe the person or persons involved probably gained access to your premises.'

'What I can't understand, inspector, is how they actually got into the building itself as everywhere is pretty much locked up overnight. The security guard would have checked everywhere at the start of his shift.'

'Well we believe, sir, they may have climbed in through an open window to gain access to the goods receiving area. In fact, when we visited the warehouse yesterday, the Gents toilet window on the ground floor was still left open. We strongly recommend you correct these deficiencies as a matter of urgency, otherwise you might be subject to another incident.'

'Well thank you, officer, for bringing this to my attention. I will certainly follow this up. So presumably you will be investigating this incident further?'

'I'm afraid not, sir. We have taken this as far as we can for the time being. If any further information comes to light then naturally we will follow it up but at this stage we are closing the incident as unsolved. We also understand the entire consignment of laptops has now been wiped clean courtesy of our High Tech Crime unit and they have now been returned to you. You will be aware, of course, that the contract has also been cancelled.'

Kevin was dumbfounded, but he was determined to find out who it was that had set this up. Could it be a disgruntled employee, a rival company or was it just pure vandalism?

***

Sunday, 20 March, 2016

The eventual security raid on "D" wing took place swiftly in the early hours of the morning when all prisoners were fast asleep in their cells. The prison security officers had decided that they should act on the information that fellow prisoner Charlie Ellis had provided as soon as possible. It was *"a case of striking while the iron was hot"* as Head of Security Tom Fletcher put it, not at first realising that they had received the tip off weeks before but hadn't even acted upon it. Early Sunday morning was the ideal time for a cell search to take place. Tariq Atiq and his cellmate Edwin Hussein were fast asleep and had wondered what on earth had hit them when at 05:00 hours, three burly prison officers marched into their cell.

Atiq and Hussein were still in a daze and made no attempt to resist. They were swiftly taken off away to the Association area while two further officers made an in-depth search of their cell. After half an hour of searching every inch of the cell, the officers left and allowed the inmates back in before deciding on which one of them would be marched off to the segregation unit. The officers didn't find any drugs that they thought they were looking for. But what they did find was something else, a mobile phone, a computer tablet together with pages of computer listings hidden inside one of the mattresses.

***

Chapter 16

HMP Dinas Bay, North Wales

Tuesday, 22 March, 2016

'So Hywel, tell me what do you make of this computer printout we recovered from that cell on "D" wing on Sunday morning?' enquired Tom Fletcher the Head of Security who was now pacing up and down in his office.

'Not a lot, sir. I'm afraid it looks like complete gobbledygook to me. It's clearly some form of computer program but I'm afraid computing is not really my specialism. I've asked one of our local computer support guys to have a look at it so we should have a better idea later on today. We have also sent the mobile phone off for examination at Tech Services. The only thing that is readable from this, however, is a list of website addresses.'

'And any joy with the computer tablet that was discovered?'

'Nothing on that at all, sir. We can't actually get into the tablet as it has a 4 digit pin number and locks out if we try too many combinations. To be honest, sir, we will probably need to send that and the paperwork off to Technical Services for specialist examination.'

'And neither Atiq or Hussein have coughed to owning any of this?'

'No, sir,' murmured Hywel, 'they are both denying any knowledge of it and said it must have been there from the previous cell occupants.'

'A bloody likely story,' yelled Tom Fletcher, 'They must think we were born yesterday. Have we had any dealings with either of them before? I mean have any of them been on report or come to our notice in any way, shape or form before?'

'Well, Atiq has been showing some signs of radicalism in the past few weeks. We think someone on his wing has been putting pressure on him. But there are no other reports that we are aware of. Both prisoners haven't presented us with any problems since they were admitted here. I wouldn't go as far as saying they are model prisoners but you can never tell with some of these.'

'OK thanks, Hywel. Please keep me informed. The governor is most interested in this little find as you can imagine.'

'Will do, sir.'

***

Kevin McNeil had taken a day off work, he was now living in his large house on his own. He had reluctantly put the ranch style house up for sale. He really was left with no option because of increasing debts and barely any income coming in and he had to cut back on all expenditure. Any savings or investments he had were now being transferred into the company to try to keep it afloat. The newspapers had been full of the demise of McNeil Industries. In fact, the local journalists seemed to thrive on keeping the story ongoing from corrupted laptops, heavy redundancies and now the alleged stealing of confidential documents. The house was the last to go and with the garden now looking overgrown, he decided he must at least try and tidy it up to make it presentable for sale. He was busy cutting the lawns and tidying the borders as best he could when his mobile phone rang. He switched off the sit-on lawnmower and took the call, it was from a withheld phone number.

'Hello, this is Kevin McNeil speaking.'

'Good morning, Mr McNeil. This is the Government Procurements department in Adelaide Terrace. We would like to arrange a meeting if you are available for this Thursday morning at 9am prompt to discuss how we might continue working together again. We have a number of potential opportunities coming up that we think you may be interested in tendering for and we are keen for competitive purposes to open these to all our local companies. Hopefully, you are available?'

'Yes, I can certainly be there,' replied Kevin eagerly who couldn't believe his ears, he thought at last maybe his luck has changed for the better and he can start rebuilding his business again.

'Excellent, I'm glad you can make it. Well you know where we are so can you please call in and ask for myself at the front desk, it's Mr V. Greene, that's G.R.E.E.N.E and I look forward to seeing you.'

Kevin thought at last a silver lining. He didn't recognise the name. But, for once in a long time, he had a smile on his face; at last, it was game on again and he was back in there.

***

Thursday, 24 March, 2016

Rob Spender was in the laboratory busy rebuilding the operating system on a corrupted force laptop, which had been hit with the ransomware bug, when the phone rang. He dropped everything and went over to his desk.

'Good morning, High Tech Crime Unit.'

'Is that the Midshire Police High Tech Crime unit?' said the voice on the other end.

'Yes, it is indeed. This is Rob Spender speaking. How can I help you?'

'Ah right, I've got the right phone number. Good morning, Rob. My name is Tony Wells from HMP Technical Services. I wonder is it possible to speak to your senior investigating officer? It is rather urgent I'm afraid.'

'Yes, I'll see if he is available, I won't keep you a moment,' replied Rob Spender as he placed the call on hold and shouted across to Jack's office.

'Jack, I've got a phone call here from someone at HMP who wishes to speak with you. Do you wish to take the call? He did say it was urgent so can I put him through?'

Jack Hodgson suddenly felt a shiver down his back at this point. Had they now discovered his previous undercover role at the prison, he also still had the prison uniform in his locker which he was hanging onto for some bizarre reason. For one minute, he nearly refused to take the call but decided that he had better speak with them.

'Erm yes, put them through, Rob. I can't think what this is about,' said Jack as he got up to close the office door.

'This is DS Jack Hodgson. How can I help you?'

'Oh hello, Jack,' came the reply, 'My name is Tony Wells. We haven't met before but I head up the technical services investigations at HMP HQ in London. I'm sorry to trouble you but we are investigating an incident at HMP Dinas Bay over in North Wales. Is now a convenient time to talk?'

Jack Hodgson's heart almost stopped, just the very mention of HMP Dinas Bay made him shudder. Maybe it did have something to do with his previous undercover role after all.

'Erm yes, that's fine and what sort of incident would that be, Tony?' he said nervously scribbling down the name and fiddling with his pen.

'Well last Sunday morning, as part of a tip off and a subsequent raid, our officers found a mobile phone, computer tablet and several program listings hidden in a mattress in a prisoner's cell. We have been tasked to investigate this and to follow it up. They also found another printout. Well, it's a handwritten note to be more precise also containing a list of website addresses. One of those website addresses is the Crime Stoppers website at Midshire Police. We felt you at least needed to know this, but we were curious as to whether you had experienced any recent attacks on that particular website and if you have what action has been taken by the force.'

Jack Hodgson couldn't believe his ears. He couldn't believe the coincidence. They'd so far drawn a blank on the ransomware investigation and here was the possible answer from Dinas Bay of all places.

'Yes, we have as a matter of fact. We had an attack a few weeks back which we have since fixed. It was a ransomware attack and we managed to limit the damage, we have quarantined the offending code. It could have been considerably worse of course but we are still investigating it here. Tell me just purely out of curiosity, do you have the names of the prisoners whose cell was raided and which wing the cell was in?'

Tony Wells was taken aback and strangely surprised why Jack Hodgson had asked such a question but decided there was no reason not to provide such information.

'We do indeed, the cell was shared by two prisoners on wing "D". I have the names here somewhere. Does the name Edwin Hussein mean anything to you?'

'No, I can't say it does. I've never heard of that name, it doesn't mean a thing to me,' replied Jack shaking his head and thinking back to when he was undercover and his incident reporting days at HMP Dinas Bay.

'Well, how about Tariq Atiq?'

'Now that name certainly does ring a bell for some reason, but I'm not sure from what.'

'Well, he was arrested by your force for credit card fraud last year apparently. Look, we do have further investigative work to carry out here but I'll keep you informed of any progress on this one. Many thanks for your help, Jack, but it does look as though Tariq Atiq could be behind this one.'

'Or Edwin Hussein of course, but yes of course, I do vaguely remember Atiq now you mention it. He was involved in a related investigation I was working on last year. Yes, please keep me informed as I think we may have a possible joint investigation here.'

'Well, you'd be most welcome to come over and join me in interviewing the pair of them if you like. Just let me know and I'll easily arrange it,' replied Tony Wells, 'I'm planning to go up there next week and naturally we would appreciate any assistance on this one.'

'Erm yes, I'll probably do that and thanks for the call. I'll get back to you later today regarding the visit to Dinas Bay,' responded Jack Hodgson thinking, *Well perhaps a visit not just yet.*

DS Hodgson replaced the receiver and sat back relaxed in the knowledge that at last they could be looking at an early result on the ransomware investigation. He thought maybe just maybe they would be finding a few answers here and for once the DCI would be pleased to hear from him. He decided to collect his thoughts before ringing the DCI. He waited until after lunch and made the phone call.

'Good morning, sir. I think we have some good news on the ransomware attacks, we have a couple of suspects…'

'Well done, Jack. I knew you would get to the bottom of this bloody Ransomware business. Just a shame it took a few weeks to pin the buggers down. So where are we with charging the offenders?' interrupted DCI Bentley as he shouted down the phone.

'Well, no one has been charged yet, sir. But I must say it does look promising. The incidents have already stopped and the various web sites affected have now been cleaned up. Our own website was one on the list of course. The odd thing is that the perpetrators appear to be from HMP Dinas Bay. An amazing co-incidence I'm sure you'll agree, sir.'

'It is indeed, Jack. So what are the next moves?'

'Well, the HMP Technical team have asked for our assistance in interviewing the two inmates Hussein and Atiq. If it's alright with you, sir, I would rather someone else make the trip to Dinas Bay. I am sure you can understand my reasoning behind this?'

'I can indeed, Jack, yes I'll ask DS Holdsworth to go up there. You can leave it to me. I think your presence there would do us no favours whatsoever, but well done again. I must admit I couldn't see an end to this lot.'

***

Kevin McNeil rose early on the Thursday morning, shaved and showered. He thought how good it was to get dressed in a suit again as for the past few weeks he'd resorted to jeans and tee shirts. He had certainly let himself go recently by not shaving and generally not looking after himself. He was keen to start rebuilding relationships again with government departments and more importantly to try and win back the business contracts he'd been losing over the past weeks and months to Gforce.

He was just about to step out of the house and head into the city when his home phone rang and he decided to take the call.

'Kevin, this is John Edmonds here. I'm sorry to ring you so early. I presume you've read in the papers the incident that I have been involved in?'

'Hi John, yes I have. You silly bugger what on earth led you to think you could get away with stealing government papers?'

'But I didn't, Kevin, I was setup. They must have been planted on my laptop, I had no idea they…'

'Don't give me that sob story,' interrupted Kevin, 'you must have known they were there.'

'No, look Kevin, I've been sacked by Gforce and we've got very little income at all now. Can you just help us out, maybe a loan to tie us over or I can come back to your place to work?'

'Sorry, John, it's your bed and you'll have to lie in it. I've got enough problems of my own.'

Kevin slammed the phone down hard and left the house mumbling to himself as he drove down to Perth. He had enough problems of his own to deal with, never mind other people's.

He arrived in the city centre at 7 am, just ahead of the peak traffic and managed to grab a leisurely coffee and croissant in a Hay Street coffee bar before walking over to Adelaide Terrace for his meeting. He'd attended many meetings before in the same building and was a familiar face to the receptionists on the front desk.

'Good morning, Mr McNeil. It's nice to see you again, how can we help you this morning?'

'Ah, good morning, Kath. Yes it's nice to be visiting here again. I have a nine o'clock meeting with Mr V. Greene in Government Procurements, he is expecting me. I guess you have a diary note of my appointment?'

The receptionist looked slightly puzzled.

'There is nothing in the diary for your meeting, but maybe he's forget to record it with us. I'm sorry what was that name again?' she replied now looking through the online address system.

'Mr V. Greene. I'm sure it's Mr V. Greene, that was the name that I had been given, he even spelt it out for me,' replied Kevin glancing down at the scrap of paper from out of his suit pocket.

'No, I'm sorry,' replied the receptionist shaking her head, 'We have no one of that name in the building, Mr McNeil. Are you sure that was the name he said?'

'Yes, I'm quite sure I wrote it down.'

'Well I'm sorry, Mr McNeil. But there is no one of that name in the building and I've also looked through the global directory which includes all the new starters.'

Suddenly Kevin McNeil realised he'd had a wasted journey but he somehow managed to hold his temper. After all there was no point in taking it out on the poor receptionist. He thought back to the call. There was something odd about it, something familiar yet he couldn't quite put his finger on it.

'Well thanks for checking, Kath. I'm really sorry to have bothered you,' said Kevin and made his way despondently out of the building.

As he walked back to his car feeling completely dejected, he hadn't noticed the young man watching his every move from the coffee bar across the street.

***

Friday, 25 March, 2016

It was the Easter weekend and the temperature was already in the thirties with a promise of a very hot day ahead. Most offices had been closed for the long weekend break. Some of the McNeil offices had now been closed, in fact, for good, never to re-open their doors again. It was now exactly a month since Kevin McNeil and Ken Diamond had been called into the government offices regarding the incident with the corrupted laptops. Good Friday it may have been, but there was nothing good about it as far as McNeil Industries were concerned. The order book had now dried up completely and a large number of staff had already been made redundant. Kevin McNeil had had no option but to also include some directors and senior management in the casualties and one of these had been Ken Diamond, the sales director. With just a few maintenance contracts to support, it was becoming increasingly difficult to keep the business afloat.

Ken and a number of employees had taken the redundancy badly. Ken had stormed out of Kevin McNeil's office when he first heard the news. Eventually, he calmed down and came back to apologise to Kevin for his behaviour. He had put in enormous efforts over the years helping Kevin to build the company up to what it had been. But there was one individual who had gone even further than Ken. That was Paul Carter from the Accounts department, who had worked for McNeil since leaving school and had worked tirelessly for the company.

Paul Carter was never really recognised for the work he did. In short, deep down he always thought he was being taken for granted and when he finally received the text telling him his services were no longer required, he flipped. He stormed out of the office block and waited for his moment after work. Kevin McNeil was just driving out of the car park when suddenly from behind the bushes; Paul pounced on the car bonnet.

'You stupid little sod,' Kevin shouted fiercely through the open window as he brought the Jaguar to a halt, 'You could have been run over, what the hell are you playing at.'

'You might have done me a favour, McNeil, if you had run me over. What chance have I got now at finding another job, you bastard? I gave you ten years of dedicated service and that's how you bloody well treat me. Well, I'll get you back for that you bloody pommie scumbag. It might take me some time but I'll get you don't you forget it!' he bawled banging hard on the car roof.

Kevin McNeil was furious and shaken at the same time as he continued driving out of the gates; in the rear mirror, he could see Paul Carter giving him numerous "V" signs as he limped off.

Other employees who had been made redundant were quite frankly glad to get out of the place, for them the writing had been on the wall over the past few weeks. Some had decided to jump ship weeks ago.

Ken Diamond however with his experience, knowledge and client contact was not out of work for long and was soon recruited by Gforce technologies as their Head of Sales and Marketing. Ken was now enjoying life in sales mode once again, wining and dining in a role he thrived in.

***

Tuesday, 29 March, 2016

DS Holdsworth jumped at the chance to get out of the office. But he'd forgotten how bad the traffic could be on a bank holiday week as he made his way slowly across the A55 dual carriageway into North Wales. He'd been stuck in the office now for the past month working on a pile of paperwork relating to a recent spate of burglaries. The storms over the weekend had been relentless. It was typical British Bank Holiday weather with many roads flooded, but it certainly hadn't stopped the holidaymakers and day trippers from venturing out. Arriving at HMP Dinas Bay an hour later than expected, he made his way hurriedly through security and was shown into the interview room where Tony Wells from HMP HQ was already waiting for him as arranged on the phone.

'Sorry I'm late, Tony. The traffic was absolutely horrendous and the wet weather didn't help at all. I lost count of the number of accidents on the way and I should have been here at least an hour ago,' said Jim Holdsworth as the two men shook hands for the first time.

'That's no problem,' replied Tony, 'Jack Hodgson told me you might be late. Anyway, it's good to meet you and I've used the spare time to familiarise myself with this particular case. You wouldn't believe the number of prison cases we have to deal with at present, most of them either involving mobile phones or drugs. I must admit we haven't come across many with computer tablets until this one. A sign of the times, I suppose.'

'Yes, I gather the smuggling in of phones has gone up drastically in the last couple of years,' responded Jim Holdsworth, 'Do you know it beats me how they even get the damn things in here.'

'Oh, you'd be surprised, Jim,' responded Tony as he was about to pick the phone up, 'They are devious buggers, they will use drones, the inside of books, milk cartons, and even inside the soles of their shoes getting them in here. I heard of one case where a prisoner in the exercise yard waited patiently for the arrival of a pigeon which had a mobile phone strapped to it. It certainly keeps our guys busy, I can tell you.'

'It's always surprised me why the prisons don't have some sort of blocking device, to zap any mobile signals. In our house you can't even make a mobile phone call, the service is so poor. I have to go to the bottom of our garden to make a bloody phone call.'

'Well that's an easy one, Jim. It causes more problems than it solves. Any blocking of signals here would interfere with our own radio transmissions, never mind the emergency services in the surrounding area.'

'Yes, I can see what you mean.'

‘Right then, shall we get started and interview Hussein first. The officers here think he’s an innocent party in all of this, they believe Atiq is the one behind this. We’ll make our own minds up of course.’

‘Yes, I remember Tariq Atiq, I interviewed him after he was arrested. A nasty piece of work as I recall who wasn’t particularly helpful in any of his interviews. By the sounds of it, he’s found his way into even more bad ways in prison.’

Tony Wells picked up the phone and dialled the security suite. He waited patiently for them to answer it which seemed to be taken hours. Eventually, it was answered and he requested them to send in Edwin Hussein as soon as possible. No more than five minutes later, an officer accompanied the prisoner who took a seat across the table from the two investigators. The prison officer took up his position and stood motionless, with hands behind his back, in front of the door pretending not to overhear the conversation that was about to take place.

‘Good morning, I’m Prison Officer Wells of HMP HQ investigation branch and this is Detective Sergeant Holdsworth of Midshire Police. We are investigating the incident recently where a number of items were found in your cell. Can we please start with your name and date of birth?’ said Tony Wells with pen poised at the ready.

‘Good morning, sir. I’m Edwin Hussein and my date of birth is 30th March 1972,’ replied the inmate politely as he continued to stand to attention.

‘So Edwin, please sit yourself down. We’d like to speak to you following the recent security raid on your cell. As you know a number of items have been found namely a computer tablet, a mobile phone and some computer listings, did any of these aforementioned items belong to yourself?’

‘No, definitely not, boss. I don’t possess any such items. I had no idea they were even there and I wouldn’t know what to do with them anyway, computing is not my thing. I have enough trouble operating a TV remote control!’

‘Had you ever seen them in the cell?’

‘No sir, never seen them before. I had no idea they were there.’

‘So have you any idea on who they might belong to?’

'No not really, presumably they belonged to Tariq. He was in the cell before me, as I say I had no idea they were even there.'

'So did you not suspect that Tariq was up to something with this tablet?'

'How could I? I hadn't seen any computer tablet. I did get suspicious that Tariq always seemed to want to spend more and more time in his cell alone and not go to association like the rest of us, presumably he was tinkering with it then.'

DS Holdsworth thought for a moment that it was a bit more than tinkering if he had been responsible for developing the ransomware bug.

'Tell me, Edwin, how do you get on with Tariq Atiq?'

'Well, we got on alright at first; we have similar backgrounds, me and him. Both of us were brought up in Manchester, had a similar education, got into some bad ways through keeping bad company. Hence we now find ourselves locked up in this bloody dump. But I'm determined to go straight after my sentence is over. I think Tariq has other ideas however. We got on really well in the beginning but I've seen a few changes in him recently. He's become angry at something or someone and I must say he's been spending quite a bit of time with some of the inmates who I think are trying to radicalise him.'

'I mean we all get depressed in here from time to time. It's only natural being locked up in here with only the fresh air in the exercise yard. Lately, I've heard him telling some of the others that when he eventually gets out of here, he's straight off to a training camp somewhere in the Middle East. I don't know which country exactly and I never showed him any interest. That's his problem if he wants to go and get himself blown up, that's his choice.'

Both DS Holdsworth and Tony Wells made notes while Edwin Hussein continued to talk about the changes that he'd noticed in Tariq Atiq over the last few months. There was clearly no love lost between the two of them.

'We can check this out of course with the prison records, Edwin, but did Tariq get many visitors as far as you were aware?' questioned the DS as he stretched his legs and walked over to the barred window.

'No, none at all that I can remember. His family gave up on him as soon as he came here. His dad runs a corner shop I think and Tariq told me that they no longer speak to each other. But I think he must have had access to some outside influence.'

'Really and what makes you say that?' replied the DS returning to his seat.

'Well, when I think about it, he must have had access to letters or maybe even emails, and Facebook or something because I remember him saying he had received some good news. God knows where he got his good news from. Nobody ever wrote to him.'

'Interesting,' murmured Tony Wells as he stroked his chin thoughtfully.

There seemed to be a long pause whilst the two investigators completed their notes in silence.

'Well, I've got nothing more to ask you, Edwin, unless DS Holdsworth still has some questions,' said Tony Wells looking over at Jim Holdsworth.

DS Holdsworth shook his head.

'Well that will be all for now, Edwin, and thanks for your time, you've been most helpful,' said Tony Wells nodding over to the prison officer to take Edwin Hussein back to his wing.

'So it looks like Tariq Atiq has some questions to answer,' said Tony Wells as soon as the door had closed.

'It does indeed and if he's as obstinate as he was last time, it will be like pulling hen's teeth!'

'Let's get him in then and see what he has to say for himself,' replied Tony as he signalled to the officer who was waiting at the door.

Ten minutes later, a somewhat dishevelled and unshaven Tariq Atiq shuffled through the doorway. He was wearing grey tracksuit bottoms, trainers and a spotless white tee shirt. He was escorted by the prison officer who had accompanied Edwin Hussein. As he approached the desk, he clearly had a memory flashback immediately recognising the DS.

'Good morning, I'm Prison Officer Wells of the HMP HQ investigation branch and this is 'Detective Sergeant Holdsworth from Midshire…'

'Yes I know who he is. I recognise him from Midshire Police,' interrupted Atiq in a threatening manner.

‘Right well, can we start with firstly confirming your name and date of birth?’ said Tony Wells calmly who was clearly used to dealing with this type of attitude from prisoners.

‘You know who I am otherwise you wouldn’t have called me in here,’ mumbled Atiq who was now slouching down in the chair.

‘Are you Tariq Atiq with a date of birth of 22nd April 1990?’

‘If you say so!’

‘So Tariq, this computer tablet that was found in your cell inside your mattress, does it belong to yourself?’ asked DS Holdsworth who was already tiring of the interview with Atiq.

‘No comment.’

‘And the computer listings that were found?’

‘No comment.’

‘So you have no idea who this computer tablet belongs to?’

‘No comment.’

‘And the mobile phone?’

‘No comment.’

‘Is there anything you would like to tell us?’

‘No comment.’

DS Holdsworth looked across at Tony Wells and nodded to each other.

‘Well clearly we are not getting anywhere here. That will be all so thank you for your lack of co-operation, which will be reported to the governor,’ said Tony Wells nodding over to the officer,’ take him away officer before I say something I shouldn’t.’

***

Monday, 11 April, 2016

Kevin McNeil at last had received some good news. He was just about to set off for work on the Monday morning when he received a call from the real estate agent in Perth. The house had finally been sold to a mystery cash buyer following the previous weekend’s open house viewing arrangements. The downside was that he would need to vacate it by the end of the month. Nevertheless, Kevin viewed this as the closing of a chapter and maybe a new beginning. Soon he would hopefully shake off the gremlins, get his life back and start trading effectively once again.

As he drove into the now almost empty car park, which months ago had been virtually full and mainly occupied by the fleet of company cars, he couldn't help noticing a hooded stranger taking photographs from a vantage point on a disused container at the end of the car park. Without even thinking, Kevin leaped out of the car leaving the engine running and spurted across the car park but before he'd even got close the stranger had vanished into thin air without a trace.

***

Tuesday, 12 April, 2016

It had been exactly two weeks since DS Jim Holdsworth had visited HMP Dinas Bay to interview Tariq Atiq and Edwin Hussein. He was now deep in discussion at a case review meeting with DCI Bentley and DS Hodgson. The case review meetings were held weekly in the DCI's office. The team were discussing the next stages and the direction of all their current cases, one of which was the joint investigation with the prison service on the Ransomware attack.

'Well there's no doubt in my mind, sir,' exclaimed DS Holdsworth, 'It has to be Atiq who is behind this and is refusing to co-operate with our enquiries. We believe he has been pocketing or at least banking the ransom demands. They are not much use to him of course whilst he is in prison but it's a fair bet he's been building up quite a substantial amount in bit coins judging by the number of attacks.'

'And we know where that lot's heading,' piped up DS Hodgson, 'probably a trip to the Middle East for terrorist training, not to mention funding the supply of weapons and ammunition . Amazing how a little computing knowledge and a wrong turn in life can lead to something like this. I mean from what I know of him, Atiq was a young law abiding individual before he got involved in all of this. He was quite well thought of running his father's shop. I think there must be someone else involved here.'

'But he's probably learnt some of those IT skills in prison, they do have IT lessons, you know,' replied the DCI, 'look, I think we need to interview our Mr Atiq again and this time I'll come with you. I think it's about time for good cop, bad cop!'

Just then the door burst open and Elizabeth Gilmore, the DCI's PA entered the office.

'I'm so sorry to disturb you, sir, but I've just taken a phone call from someone called Tony Wells at HMP HQ. He left an urgent message for DS Holdsworth to say that he's received a call from HMP Dinas Bay. He told me to tell you that Tariq Atiq has been found dead in his cell, apparently he has hung himself.
'

'Well that's saved us a journey,' replied the DCI somewhat sarcastically, 'the point is now, gentlemen, where do we go from here?'

'Well, sir, as I was saying,' interrupted DS Hodgson, 'I think someone else has had to have been helping him with this, boss. I remember Atiq from my time in Dinas Bay and I can't see him doing this on his own. To be honest, he's not clever enough if you ask me. No, there is someone else involved in this. It could be someone in the prison but it's definitely someone who knows his way around a keyboard.'

'But who, that is the question.'

***

Part 2

Chapter 17

Monday, 4 July, 2016

The Western Australian winter had now arrived and the temperatures had dropped significantly. At the start of the working week, it was cold, wet, windy and miserable. But even in this rainiest month of the year in Western Australia, the sun can continue to shine although today had been one of the wettest on record. Kevin McNeil was driving home from work through a sudden downpour of intensive rain, which slowed the evening traffic on the freeway down to almost a standstill. It was nearly four months now that had passed since McNeil Industries had hit huge problems in trading.

The company was now a shadow of its former self. Gone were all the retail branches in the other states and the main Asia Pacific electronics warehouse in Jandakot had also closed down. Kevin had somehow managed to keep part of the business going with only a skeleton staff. All the big ideas in online trading, huge warehouse developments and the Asia Pacific expansion plans were all a distant memory and had all gone. All that was left now was the old dilapidated Fremantle warehouse and adjacent office block together with a small number of back street electronic gadget shops in Western Australia. He had been forced to sell the main head office building and he now occupied a shabby little office in the warehouse itself. Gforce Technologies had picked up most of the new business, and they were now well, and truly, the new kid on the block, the big player in town.

A large number of McNeil's employees had also managed to find work there. Kevin, however, was determined to try and rebuild the company to the level it had been before but deep down he knew he was onto a losing battle. With his ranch style house in The Vines also gone, he was now renting a small house near Armadale about a forty-minute drive from Perth. The flash cars, the yacht and all the trappings of a luxury lifestyle were all gone. He was now working twelve hours a day for next to nothing and on this particular evening, he had arrived home depressed and exhausted. He parked his car on the roadside and ran into the house trying to escape the torrential rain.

In just the short distance from the car to the house, he was wringing wet through. He'd worked right through the weekend looking for every business opportunity he could find but had nothing to show for it. He thought to himself, *How could it have possibly come to this and in only just a few months*. He went into the small lounge at the rear of the property, dried himself off and switched on the TV. He then slumped down to watch the latest Channel Nine news which included a news item on Gforce Technologies which didn't seem to help him at all. Kevin poured himself a large whisky and that was also another one of his problems. He had now resorted to heavy drinking, drinking to the point where he would regularly collapse in the armchair each evening having finished an entire bottle of whisky. As he dropped off to sleep, he didn't notice the small camera perched high above the curtain rail watching his every move.

***

Western Australia Courier - 4 July, 2016

The government today announced the completion of phase 1 of Project Watchman the controversial emergency services initiative which has been under development since it first received approval for funding earlier this year. The project has in fact been designed over the past few years pending funding for the implementation of Phase 1. The first phase which covers selected areas of Perth city centre and Fremantle has today been switched on by the Head of Government Services Phil Pleasance who made the following statement today.

"We are pleased today to officially announce the switching on of a new investigative support system which has been designed to assist our hard working emergency services in the detection and investigation of incidents in our region.

The design and development of the new system has in fact taken years of careful planning and will enable officers to gather visual and data evidence of scenes immediately prior to and during specific incidents. I am sure you will appreciate that considerable investment has been made in both hardware and software and we are confident that this offers our region a major step change in the investigation and detection of crimes. I would also like to take this opportunity to thank the development team who have done an amazing job delivering Phase 1 on time and within budget."

However, Frank Carstairs spokesman of the protest group BBWatchman, when interviewed later commented, "We still have real serious concerns and misgivings regarding the implementation of this system particularly not only with the way data is captured but the way it is stored and archived. The harvesting of data on this grand scale is a major concern to us. For example, it is estimated that over a year, many billions of records will be added to this database and without proper archiving and deletion control; this will lead to incorrect information being used in investigations. I don't think the general public realise how serious this could be. Just imagine if this information is out of date or incorrect it could lead to tragic consequences."

***

DS Jack Hodgson had just completed his six month assignment with the High Tech Unit and had now packed up his bags and returned to the CID team which was now based in the Midshire Police Headquarters.

He'd learnt a great deal from the guys in the High Tech Unit but was certainly glad to be back in CID as he'd felt at times like a duck out of water managing "*The Techies*" as he called them. In fairness, they had all worked very well together overall but the return of their boss DS Williams from long term sick meant that Jack could now return to the CID fold.

For the time being, Jack now directly reported to DCI Bentley himself and he was involved in assisting him with the future crime strategy project in Police HQ. It was a cushy desk number with normal hours but it did have its downside particularly as his desk was immediately outside the DCI's office.

***

Monday, 18 July, 2016

With Phase One of Project Watchman now completed and after the grand switching on ceremony, the trials had commenced in earnest at the selected secret locations throughout the region. Investigating officers in those locations had been informed that they had the support of the system and had been actively encouraged to use the data in their investigations if needed. All had gone remarkably smoothly and the development team had now moved onto getting ready for the next phase, the electronic link between the driver licensing database and the sat nav traffic monitoring.

First indications showed that already on Phase One police officers in the areas that were supported by the trial were starting to find the system invaluable in the investigation and early detection of crimes. However, an increasing number of members of the public continued to raise their concerns and felt uneasy at what they saw as a big brother approach. The government had made a big splash in the media on how the development was unique in Australia and how interest was also forthcoming from all over the world. Adam Taylor was kept even busier than normal and was already receiving phone calls, emails and enquiries from a number of Police forces worldwide.

***

The development team on Project Watchman had decided to have their own grand ceremony to celebrate their completion of Phase One. Immediately after work on the Monday evening, they planned to head over to the many Northbridge bars and nightclubs. The team all got on well together and had a 'work hard, play hard' philosophy. Most weekends, there would be a social gathering of some description but it was unusual for them to have a drinking session on a Monday evening. A number of them had already booked the following day off just as a precaution. So at 5pm on the dot, the project director assembled his team in the reception area.

'Right, guys, now listen up, let's enjoy this sundowner. The first round of drinks is on me and you've all earned this for a job, well done,' said Adam Taylor with a large grin on his face.

An almighty cheer went up around the reception area.

'I did say only the first round, guys. Now look, we meet as soon as possible at the Elephant and Wheelbarrow pub in Northbridge and we'll decide there where we are going to eat later on. Anyone not planning to be there, well you'd better have a really good excuse ready. I'm afraid a note from your mum will not do on this occasion!'

Paul had however decided not to join the team that evening as he had too many other things on his mind. Just as they were heading out, he approached Adam as he was about to jump in a waiting taxi.

'I'm sorry, Adam, I can't make it tonight I'm afraid. I'll have to join you another time. I have a really bad migraine and need to go home,' he lied,' I just need to go and have a lie down, I hope you will understand, hopefully I can make it next time.'

'No problem, Paul, you get yourself sorted out. You've spent too much time in front of that PC monitor. I'll catch you in the morning all being well.'

Paul Arrowsmith had other plans that evening and he certainly needed a clear head.

***

Kevin McNeil was still at work thinking through his long-term plan of survival. He was determined to somehow get the business back to what it was, but it was going to take some considerable time. The business he'd worked so hard to build up for the last decade and he was prepared to go to any lengths to get it back on track. He had a few ideas and if all went to plan, he could be well on the way to financial stability once again, regaining his credibility and the client base in the process. He was the last one to leave the office on the Monday evening. After checking everywhere to make absolutely sure he was actually the last person in the building, he picked up his briefcase, switched all the lights off and locked up the other doors in the warehouse. There was no requirement for a night watchman or security guard any more. There was nothing really worth stealing in the warehouse and it was also one less salary to pay.

He always worked late these days, not that there was plenty of work but he had no real reason for going home. There was no one there to greet him or look after him. He was now living a very lonely life style indeed. He had lost his so-called friends and had no real interests outside work. Here was a sad and lonely figure who at times had also lost all his confidence. As he made his way through to his battered old car in the car park, he stopped momentarily to look back at the warehouse. He had all sorts of ideas running through his head and thought, *There has to be another way*. He drove through the gates then put the padlock on the old rusty metal gates.

He called in at a takeaway on the way home. He'd now also resorted to fast food takeaways and it was also beginning to show on the old waistline. Paul ate his burger and fries, sat in the car in the car park feeling very sorry for himself. He had to keep telling himself he could get through this but only if he was strong enough. He thought, *It's just another hiccup, another cruel test that life throws at you*. When he eventually arrived home later that night, totally exhausted, he got changed into his pyjamas and dressing gown and settled down for the evening. Once again he hit the whisky bottle and soon he was fast asleep in the armchair.

Kevin McNeil was now sound asleep and snoring loudly still slumped in the armchair. Suddenly in the middle of his dream, he could hear a telephone ringing continuously. He tried to dismiss it and put it out of his mind continuing to snore on but it continued and eventually he woke from his slumbers. He leaned over, switched on the table lamp and glanced at the wall clock. It was just after 2am, the mobile on the coffee table continued to ring and he reluctantly answered it.

'Is that Mr McNeil of McNeil Industries?' came the voice on the other end.

'Yes, speaking. Who is this and what bloody time do you call this ringing me at this hour of the morning?'

'I'm very sorry to disturb you, Mr McNeil, but this is Senior Sergeant Mann at Fremantle Police station here. It is rather urgent and I'm afraid I have some bad news. I'm sorry to tell you that your warehouse in Fremantle is on fire. The fire service is in attendance and with a bit of luck will have it under control very soon. I don't have any further details at this point but under the circumstances I suggest you…'

'That's dreadful news, officer, this is like a bad dream. Look, I'll get dressed immediately and get down there,' interrupted Kevin McNeil and replaced the receiver before the officer had even finished his sentence.

Chapter 18

Tuesday, 19 July, 2016

Kevin McNeil couldn't believe the sight before him as he drove his old Nissan Micra in the direction of the Fremantle warehouse. As he approached the area, he could already see huge flames and smoke leaping high into the early morning sky. He arrived there just before 3am and could see the building was well ablaze with flames and the blue lights of emergency vehicles lighting up the windows of the surrounding properties. The car park and adjacent streets had all been sealed off by the police and he had no option but to park in the housing estate several hundred yards up the road. He could see a number of residents being hurriedly escorted by the police into a nearby sports hall. As he walked back to the warehouse, he was approached in the smoke at the barriers by a solitary police officer.

'Sorry sir, I'm afraid this is as far as you can go. It's far too dangerous for anyone to go in there. I suggest you follow the residents into the sports hall down the street. You'll be quite safe in there and you can get a hot drink,' said the officer placing an arm out in front him.

'But I don't live around here I am the owner of the warehouse, officer.'

'That's as maybe, sir. But I'm afraid I've had my orders and been told not to let anyone near the crime scene, no one at all. I'm sure you can understand that, sir. My instructions are quite clear.'

'Crime scene, what do you mean crime scene?'

‘Well, it appears the warehouse has been deliberately set alight sir and the fire service and police investigation teams are on site now. Vandalism if you ask me, we are seeing an increase in this type of incident. You’d think they’d have better things to do with their time. No one is allowed anywhere near there, it’s also for your own safety, sir. I suggest you return home and come back in the morning. I am sure our investigation team will want to talk with you then.’

Kevin McNeil was about to answer the officer back and insist on seeing his senior officer but he decided after careful thought to return home. There was nothing he could do here anyway and besides he’d only just remembered that he was still the worse for wear and would have been well over the limit if they had breathalysed him. As he drove back, he kept thinking about the officer’s remarks on it being a crime scene and the lengths some people will go to. He reflected on what sort of person would do such a thing.

***

Paul Arrowsmith had also not slept well that night as he had far too much on his mind working through the final stages of his plan. His mind was now buzzing with options, had he thought everything through, one little mistake and the plan would be over. But everything was now in place for the grand finale. Soon if all goes to plan, he would be able to head out of Australia, collect his ill-gotten gains and maybe step back into being Tim Ridgway once again. He had his heart set on making a fresh start in a new land.

***

Kevin McNeil had returned to his rented place back at Armadale. The roads in the early hours were naturally empty at that time of day and he arrived back home in record time. He was dog tired and climbed into bed, still dressed in his clothes, around 3:30am but try as he might, he just couldn’t get off to sleep. He resorted once again to the whisky bottle to see if that would knock him out and eventually, he dozed off around 7:30am but was awakened by the doorbell shortly after 8:15. He turned over and tried to ignore it but the ringing of the bell and the incessant banging on the door continued. Eventually with bleary eyes, he crawled out of bed and made his way downstairs. On opening the door, he vaguely recognised the two men standing before him but he couldn't quite place them.

'Good morning, Mr McNeil. We are sorry to disturb you but we have a number of questions we need to ask you. I'm Inspector Randall and this is my colleague Sergeant Brown from Fremantle Police, may we come in?'

Kevin McNeil remembered exactly at that moment where he had seen them before. These were the same two police officers who had interviewed him a while back at his offices about the laptop incident. He thought for a second whether he should ask them to come back later as he had had very little sleep all night. In the end, he decided it wouldn't take too long and at least he could then get some shut eye.

'Yes, please come in and sit yourselves down. Excuse the mess, I haven't had time to tidy up yet.' The two officers followed him into the small partially furnished lounge area. As they entered the room, Inspector Randall and Sergeant Brown glanced at each other, they could smell smoke on Kevin McNeil's clothes.

'Please take a seat,' prompted Kevin McNeil slurring his words and pointing to the settee.

'No, that's fine, sir. If we can just ask you a few questions and my sergeant here will take a few notes.'

'How can I help, officer?'

'Firstly, have we been drinking, sir?' asked the inspector.

'Just a nightcap afraid I'm afraid I couldn't sleep,' responded Kevin McNeil who was now having difficulty even speaking clearly, 'there's no law against it in your own home, is there?'

'No, none at all, sir. Now if you don't mind we'll continue.'

'Yes no problem, go right ahead. I assume this is about last night's fire at the warehouse?' asked Kevin who was now looking somewhat anxious.

'Yes, that's right, Mr McNeil. We presume you have heard the news about your warehouse,' said the inspector looking slightly puzzled.

'Yes, that's right. I returned to the warehouse earlier this morning, but there was nothing I could do so I came back home.'

'Can you please confirm the time you left the warehouse premises last night after work?' enquired the inspector who was already somewhat surprised that Kevin already knew about the warehouse fire.

'Erm, yes I suppose, let me see that would be about 8:30 last night.'

'And were you the last person to leave the building?'

'I was indeed, yes. I checked that everyone had gone home before locking up. I then checked all the doors, set the burglar alarm, locked the building and finally the car park gates then made my way home.'

'Did you drive straight home, sir?'

'Erm, no I needed something to eat and I called into a Harry's fast food restaurant for a takeaway just off the Kwinana Freeway and then I went straight home.'

'So let's see, assuming that the traffic would have been light around that time, you would have arrived at home, let's say about 9:30pm, is that right?'

'Yes, it would be about then, officer.'

'So can you account for your time after 9:30pm?'

'I was at home having a drink.'

'And can anyone confirm that, I mean were you with anyone at home?'

'No, I was on my own. Look, what is all this about, inspector?'

'Well, sir, we have reason to believe that you may have come back to the warehouse around midnight.'

'What you must be mistaken and for what purpose?' suddenly realising that he was being accused of burning down his own warehouse.

The two officers were silent.

'Are you suggesting, officer, that I started the fire?'

'Well, sir, I noticed you used the word "*returned*" and we do have someone answering your description who according to our information was driving a Nissan Micra away from the scene shortly after midnight. We couldn't help noticing in your driveway that you drive a Nissan Micra. Bit of a coincidence that, don't you think?'

'That's ridiculous, why on earth would I do such a thing and in any case there are thousands of Nissan Micras on the road?'

'Well it has been known before, sir, say for insurance purposes.'

'Look this is crazy, officer. I've nothing to gain whatsoever.'

'Well, sir, I'm afraid we will have to continue this conversation down at the station so please get your things together and we'll carry on our conversation down there.'

'But this is preposterous; I haven't done anything wrong. Am I under arrest?'

'No, of course not, but we'd like you to come back with us, Mr McNeil, just to clear a few things up.'

'I want to call my solicitor!'

'All in good time, we can soon clear this up at the station, sir, now if you don't mind,' replied the inspector taking a firm hold of Kevin McNeil's arm.

***

The Midshire Police in the UK were also aware of the innovative development in Western Australia which had received wide publicity not just in Australia but within the Criminal Justice sector globally. The Watchman project now featured in a number of Law Enforcement magazines and was quickly gaining worldwide interest. The future crime strategy project team chaired by DCI Bentley had also shown great interest in the project down under. Jack Hodgson was busy at his desk writing a report for the Assistant Chief Constable (Crime) on the benefits of residents performing their own online crime reporting when he was called into the DCI's office.

'Jack, have you seen this Australian article? What do you think?' said the DCI handing him a copy of the latest Law Enforcement magazine.

'I have, yes sir, I read it the other day and it's very ambitious if you ask me. I think it may be a step too far but good luck to them all the same, they will certainly need it.'

'I agree, ambitious it maybe but with more than our fair share of CCTV and speed, sorry safety cameras throughout the force, I'm really keen to learn if it could be possibly adapted in our own area. Now look, Jack, I'd like you to contact the Watchman development team in Australia and see what you can find out. This could put us on the map you know. Now you must excuse me I must get over to see the ACC, see what you can find out and keep me informed. I should be back after lunch,' remarked the DCI as he left the office in a hurry.

Jack Hodgson didn't quite share the DCI's enthusiasm for Project Watchman. He could see the benefits but even if they had the required funding, he could also see all sorts of issues implementing something similar in the force. After re-reading the article, he decided to give the WA project team a call. In British Summer Time with only a seven-hour time difference between the UK and Western Australia at this time of the year, it was easy for him to make contact with them. Jack decided in the first instance to contact the project director Adam Taylor by phone. He decided, rather than wait; he would strike while the iron was hot and catch him before he left the office for home. He was in luck.

'Good afternoon, you are through to the Project Watchman team, Adam Taylor speaking. How can I be of assistance?'

'Hello Adam, we haven't met before. My name is DS Jack Hodgson at Midshire Police in the UK. I recently read the press article on Project Watchman and we are keen as a force to find out more about it. I understand that you are the project director of the Watchman project?'

'Yes, that's correct, Jack. News travels fast and I must say we've been inundated with requests for information already and particularly from the UK forces. So how can I help you exactly?'

'Well, we are very interested in knowing more about your project and we have been following its progress which we understand is now live. We realise it's still early days yet but we believe there is scope for the same type of solution over here. I wonder if you could please send me any background information that you may have, something which puts a bit more flesh on the press release document so to speak. As I say, I am sure it's still a bit early for the pros and cons of the project as I guess it is still undergoing trials but anything you can let me have, I'd appreciate. Naturally, it will be treated in complete confidence, of course.'

'Yes, certainly Jack, there are just a couple of things that I should mention. First, it is only Phase One that has gone live at this stage and we do have much bigger plans for this, providing we can get the necessary funding of course, which might be tricky. You are right though, we haven't by any means evaluated the pros and cons of this project yet, that will come much later in a report which we will be releasing. In the meantime, I do have a more detailed press pack that I can send you, which I think you will find helpful. I suggest you email me first and I'll get this to you. You can always call me back if you need more information of course or if you just want to discuss any aspect of it. We are always happy to help our UK colleagues.'

'Excellent, Adam, that will be most useful and a good start in getting to understand the project. I have your email address so I will get back in touch straight away and thanks again for your help.'

As Jack Hodgson replaced the receiver, he thought, *Maybe there's a trip down under on the horizon. I mean after all you have to see these things first hand. You can't really appreciate them from a distance even though it might mean sitting next to the DCI on a plane for over twenty hours!*

He typed up a quick email to Adam Taylor confirming their phone call and his request for information. He couldn't have expected a faster response to his enquiry. Minutes later he received the press pack from Perth, which he immediately forwarded onto the DCI's email address. Just a shame, the DCI filed it for later consideration.

***

'So let me get this straight, Mr McNeil. You say you were at home all evening on your own from 9:30pm and you had a few drinks, then dropped off to sleep in the armchair. The next thing you remember is getting a phone call from one of our officers who you say is apparently based here at the Fremantle Police Station.'

'Yes officer, that's correct.'

'So you then got dressed in the middle of the night and drove straight down to the warehouse, is that correct?'

'Yes, that's right. Look I keep telling you it was an officer from this very police station who rang me. I just can't remember his name, for god's sake, why don't you believe me?'

'I want to believe you, sir, but we have no trace whatsoever of any phone call to yourself. True, we did try ringing the key holder as soon as we were alerted about the fire, but the number was unobtainable. The only number we have on our key holder database is a landline number in "The Vines" area.'

'Well that would have probably been my old telephone number. I moved out of there a while ago. If you give me a moment, I'll remember the officer's name. I remember it was a senior sergeant.'

'Come on, Mr McNeil, I wasn't born yesterday. There was no phone call was there? Like a number of criminals, you returned to the scene around 3:00 am out of curiosity to witness the damage you had done earlier on.'

'That's complete rubbish, why on earth would I do such a thing?'

'You tell me, but from what I gather business hasn't been going too well for you lately and maybe the insurance had something to do with it. Think how much you would gain from that.'

Kevin McNeil thought for a moment and then suddenly wondered if he even had a current insurance policy on the building. Jane Patterson used to deal with all those matters and she'd been made redundant months ago.

'You seem to have gone quiet, Mr McNeil, perhaps you'd like to get this lot off your chest, you might feel better then,' prompted Sergeant Brown who had remained silent until this point.

'But I haven't done anything, you are totally mistaken. I keep telling you I had a call from one of your officers in the early hours of this morning. If you just give me a moment, I should be able to give you a name.'

'Take all the time you like, Mr McNeil, we are not going anywhere and neither for that matter are you. Let's face it, there was no officer who called you, nor any phone call was there. We have no record of this call whatsoever. You set fire to your own warehouse, is that right?'

'No, I keep telling you, I had nothing to do with the fire.'

Kevin was trying desperately hard to remember who it was who called him. Just then from nowhere Kevin then remembered from the phone call the officer's name.

'That's it,' replied Kevin McNeil as he thumped the table in anger, 'it was Senior Sergeant Mann, yes that was the name he gave me. Just ask him, go on, contact him now, Senior Sergeant Mann. He'll confirm exactly what I'm telling you.'

Both police officers shook their heads in disbelief and looked blank at each other.

'I'm sorry but we don't have anyone with that name, Mr McNeil. I've been based at Fremantle police station now for ten years and I know everyone here. I can tell you now that there is no officer by that name. Now look we've wasted enough time on this already so I suggest that you cool off and we'll continue this conversation later on. Sergeant, can you please escort Mr McNeil to the Custody suite? It might just give him enough time for him to recall his memory!'

***

WA Courier – Wednesday, 20 July, 2016

'Police Treating Cause of Blaze at Warehouse as Suspicious'

A large Fremantle warehouse was virtually destroyed in a huge fire in the early hours of Tuesday morning with arson being the possible cause. A spokesman for the police service tweeted that the warehouse owned by McNeil Industries and used for the storage of electrical components was set alight between the hours of midnight and 3am.

Glen Baxter, supervisor for the Fremantle Fire Service said, "At the height of the blaze, there were five crews attending the scene and they had worked tirelessly around the clock to bring the fire under control."

An official press release from the police service states, "Thankfully no one has been injured in the fire and at this stage, the cause of the blaze is unknown. However, I can confirm a man is being held in custody assisting us with our enquiries."

***

Chapter 19

Thursday, 21 July, 2016

Kevin McNeil arrived home by taxi in the early hours of the Thursday morning. He was exhausted having spent all of yesterday and most of the night being questioned by detectives over the arson attempt on his warehouse. For now, he was being released without charge pending further investigations into the actual cause of the blaze at his Fremantle warehouse. He had never felt so low. He'd lost his wife, his family, thc house and now his business, all within six months. He was in a desperate situation and could not see how he could possibly continue with a business with no premises.

Short on sleep and looking much the worse for wear, he stumbled through his front door and picked up the bundle of letters lying on the doormat, which had just been delivered. He could quickly see they were mostly junk mail or bills. But there was one letter in particular that stood out, a neatly typed envelope bearing a local postmark addressed to him, personally care of McNeil Industries. He wondered how the sender had even known his personal address and why it hadn't been delivered to the office address.

Curious, he discarded all the other mail on the hall table, ripped open the envelope and started reading the contents. Inside was a typed letter, it was short but to the point. As he quickly scanned the letter, suddenly his face lit up, at last a bit of good news, an invite out of the blue, which certainly brightened up his day.

He read it again just to make sure he hadn't misread it.

***

Friday, 22 July, 2016

Kevin McNeil was up bright and early on the Friday morning, he had spent most of yesterday catching up on much needed sleep. He had been told in no uncertain terms not to visit the warehouse on the Thursday, as the investigators would be still at the scene and they would be looking for clues as to the source of the fire. He decided, however, on the Friday to take a chance and revisit the warehouse to see the extent of the damage. As he arrived at the gate, he could see the building was still smouldering but was surprised to see that there were also two police officers still guarding the entrance. He parked the car in the side road and approached one of the officers on duty.

'Good morning, officer. I'm the owner of this warehouse and wondered if I may now access my own premises? I have some documents that I need to recover urgently,' said Kevin showing him his driving licence and expecting to be shown straight through the barriers.

'Well I'll need to check, Mr McNeil, as I do have instructions not to let anyone through, just a minute. I won't keep you a moment,' replied the officer who for some reason then walked off to radio through to the investigation team for confirmation.

Moments later, he returned to the barriers.

'Yes, that will be fine, Mr McNeil. Just go straight ahead. Be careful where you walk and Inspector Wolfe will meet you there at the office entrance.'

Kevin McNeil walked through the car park, which was now littered with debris. He couldn't believe his eyes, most of the goods receiving and large warehouse areas were reduced to rubble. Clearly, the main building had now collapsed with crumbling brick walls standing proud into the sky like some odd modern sculpture. Still standing, however, with the roof intact was the charred remains of the office and the old canteen area. He stepped over a number of twisted metal girders and broken roof tiles. The car park was littered with broken glass and rubble and in the distance he could see a police officer waiting for him.

As he got closer, he could see the inspector waiting for him at what was left of the charred entrance to the offices.

'Good morning, sir. It's Mr McNeil, I believe,' said the inspector politely, 'I'm afraid it's not looking too good as you can see the fire service have managed to confine the blaze to the warehouse area, but they did manage to save the office area as best they could. I'm afraid, however, we still cannot let you near there, not just for your own safety but the forensic teams have not yet finished and I'm sorry to remind you, sir, but you have been released pending further investigations. I'm sure you can understand why you cannot go any further.'

'Yes I quite understand, this is like a bad dream, inspector. Look, is there any chance I can get access to the documents in the office or at least have them removed from there. That way I can at least try and conduct some sort of business continuation from home?'

'Well, I'll see what we can do, sir. As the windows blew out, there is a considerable amount of glass dust in there as you can imagine and any documents that have been left on desks etc. will either have been burnt or will need to be sanitised first. So I suggest you forget about those. Anything filed in cabinets should be OK so leave it with me and I'll see what we can do. It may take some time though I'm afraid.'

'Thank you, officer, well here is my business card with my home address. I'd appreciate access to any of my documents that you can retrieve, see what you can do.'

Kevin McNeil returned to his car, there was nothing further he could do back there. In the meantime, he had a number of phone calls to make to the remains of his existing customer base and also confirm that he will take up the opportunity that he had received in the recent letter. But first, he had the most important call of all and that was to Jane Paterson.

***

The Arson investigation team from the WA Fire and Rescue service had just completed their initial forensic analysis of the scene at the Fremantle warehouse. They were now gathered at Fremantle Police station for a meeting with Inspector Wolfe and Sergeant Kelly from CID. Fire Investigation Officer Rob Carney chaired the meeting and presented the squad's findings to the two police officers.

'Thanks for coming over so quickly, Rob,' said Inspector Wolfe who was keen to get the arson investigation off the ground, 'so what can you tell us from your initial findings?'

'Well, it's definitely arson and whoever started this fire wanted to make sure of the extent of damage. The seat of the fire has been identified as starting in the goods receiving area where we have found evidence that petrol was involved. There is no doubt about it, this was a deliberate act to do extensive damage. The fire would have escalated rapidly igniting all of the cardboard boxes and the electronic equipment that was stored there. We reckon at its height, the temperature would have reached over 850 centigrade in there.'

'What I can't understand, Rob, is that there was no fire alarm, no call into the control room, nothing. If it hadn't been for a passing motorist we wouldn't have even been alerted.'

'Well that's interesting you say that. You are right of course. The flames and smoke would have set off the smoke detectors and fire alarms early on but these appear not to have been working. In fact, on close examination of the charred remains of the detectors, we observed they were at least 15 years old. They should have been replaced well before they were ten years old.'

'Incidentally, did you finally manage to identify the motorist?' said Rob inquisitively 'rumour has it that he or she rang off, which I find quite odd.'

'That's something we are still working on,' said Sergeant Kelly, 'we have a number of witness statements that we need to go through in fine detail. As yet we haven't identified him. It was a man's voice apparently. What I can't get over, Rob, is how fast this fire took hold. I mean the emergency services were there within five minutes of the anonymous phone call and the place was well alight.'

'Of course we don't know how long it had been going when the anonymous caller rang in,' replied Rob, 'it wouldn't take long to get established. As the fire progressed through the warehouse, the glass in the windows would have been shattered and these openings would also have contributed to driving the heat and smoke more rapidly through the building.'

***

'Jane, is that you?'

'Yes. Kevin how nice to hear from you after all this time. I'm really sorry to hear about your troubles but I imagine you are on top of things. Are things sorting themselves out at last?'

'No, I'm afraid not, Jane, they have got considerably worse if anything. I've now lost the warehouse, I don't know if you have heard but we've been hit with a huge fire and it's destroyed the place.'

'Oh, that's terrible, Kevin, I'm so sorry. Was anyone injured, are you alright?'

'No, no one was injured thankfully. There was no one in there at the time. It was overnight early on Tuesday morning. Look, Jane, I was wondering do you have the details of the insurance company that we have our policy with? I cannot get access to the office and I need to contact them urgently.'

'Well no, I haven't, Kevin,' Jane hesitated, 'can't you remember you decided not to renew the policy back in February as they had significantly increased the premium. We were going to get another set of insurance quotes from other companies. You told me not to renew it!'

Kevin's heart sank. Suddenly, he'd remembered the conversation they had. There had been so much going on at the time he had completely forgotten about the renewal with so much on his mind.

'Oh God, yes. I remember.'

'Oh Kevin, don't tell me you didn't take out another insurance policy, is there nothing you can do?'

'Oh Jane, I don't think I can stand much more of this, its bad news after bad. Look, I'll call you back later.'

***

The Midshire Police ACPO ranks (Association of Chief Police Officers) were in deep discussion in the board room reviewing the past six months' crime statistics that had just been released. The figures did not make for good reading, although the general level of crime reporting was down across the force area the detection rate left a lot to be desired.

‘Well gentlemen, you can see for yourselves. We were in a much better shape this time last year compared with the same period this year,’ remarked the Chief Constable, ‘Crimes are down but so is our detection rate, so, Mr Redmain, what do you propose to do about it?’

Trevor Redmain was the newly appointed Assistant Chief Constable (Crime) for Midshire Police and one of the youngest ACCs in the force. He had been in the police service for over fifteen years and had come through the ranks with flying colours following graduating from Nottingham University. He had been in CID for five years and had impressed the powers that be particularly as he had been a successful senior investigating officer on a number of difficult serial cases.

Trevor Redmain thought for a moment, he didn’t want to rock the boat but decided to go for it anyway.

‘Well sir, I think it’s time as a force that we moved out of the 20th century. We have been stuck in our ways for too long now and we should learn from some of the innovative projects that we are hearing about worldwide,’ responded ACC Redmain, ‘Let me give you an example. There is one development in particular which has come to our notice. You may have read about it yourselves, and that is Project Watchman which is being trialled in Australia and is already receiving wide acclaim. As I say, we seem to have been stuck in a rut with our old traditional methods here and I’m afraid to say the world has moved on.’

‘And do you have details of this so called Watchman project, Mr Redmain?’ demanded the Chief Constable who had only twelve months left to serve and certainly didn’t want to leave under a cloud introducing something, last of all, which would affect his departure. He was sceptical, but nevertheless open to new ideas.

‘We do indeed, sir, I shall ask DCI Bentley to circulate the project briefing pack to everyone for consideration. My understanding is that we received a set of documents quite recently.’

‘Excellent, I shall look forward to reading that, Trevor. I agree with you it is about time we moved with the times and anything we can learn from other forces will of course be beneficial.’

The Chief Constable thought to himself, *And with a bit of luck, I'll be retired and out of here long before this gets implemented.*

***

Monday, 25 July, 2016

McNeil had spent all weekend ringing around his old business contacts looking for work and any opportunity or even the possibility of new business. He'd drawn a blank, no one was interested. Word had got around that McNeil was struggling. Even his old business partner Ken Diamond hadn't bothered to return his phone calls. Once again, Kevin had resorted to drowning his sorrows with the whisky bottle at his side. All he had left now was the possibility of what had been described as a significant business opportunity in the mysterious letter that he'd just received. The letter had asked him to view a unique demonstration which was taking place at 2 pm on Friday, 29 July at a warehouse just outside Kewdale. The letter was unsigned and normally Kevin McNeil would have tossed it straight in the waste bin but he was desperate, he'd consider anything. These were exceptional times and he kept telling himself, maybe just maybe my luck will change tomorrow and sure enough it did, but for the worse.

Chapter 20

Tuesday, 26 July, 2016

Inspector Wolfe and Sergeant Kelly were now poring over the few witness statements they had received relating to the arson attack on the Fremantle Warehouse blaze.

'This vehicle sighting looks most interesting around midnight, boss,' said Sergeant Kelly, 'if we could just get more of a camera angle on the vehicle and identify the registration. I think it could prove useful. It may not be involved of course but at least we can eliminate it. We know it's a Nissan Micra but according to the Department of Transport, there are over six thousand of those that are registered in Perth alone.'

'I've been thinking, Sergeant, on this, have you checked whether that new Project Watchman covers any of this area? We could very well find if it does we've got more information available to us. Can you get onto the Watchman monitoring team as soon as possible and see if they can provide us with anything?

'Never used it, sir, but yes I guess it's worth a try.'

***

'Jack, I need a favour. The ACC Crime has asked for a copy of that press briefing pack on that Watchman project down in Australia. Can you dig it out for me, print it off, there's a good chap and bring it in if you would? I assume we have received it by now?' requested DCI Bentley as he returned to his office.

'Yes, I did send it to you last week, sir, but I can soon find it again for you,' responded DS Hodgson who was by now quite used to the DCI misplacing documents.

'Did you? Well I never had time to read it. Too much pressure and all that but it appears the ACC has it in mind that we should be taking a closer look at it.'

DS Hodgson set about locating the email and printed the document from his inbox. He collected the fifteen page printout from the printer and took it straight into the DCI's office.

'Here we are, sir. It's quite detailed but it should give us a better appreciation of it, still a bit ambitious if you ask me,' said DS Hodgson handing over the document and returning to his desk.

The DCI opened up the document and started leafing through the pages. His eyes were drawn almost immediately to a photograph which was part way through the introduction. Jack Hodgson had just sat down at his desk when he heard this almighty shout coming from the DCI's office.

'Jack, come in here quick and ask DS Holdsworth to come with you pronto, as soon as you can,' boomed the DCI.

DS Holdworth and DS Hodgson raced into the DCI's office wondering what on earth could have happened.

'Have you seen this? Does anyone look familiar on here?' shouted the DCI pointing to the photograph in front of them, 'Here!'

The two sergeants peered over at a photograph of the Watchman development team in standing in front of Police HQ. They were celebrating at an event after completing Phase 1 ahead of schedule.

'Bloody hell, I don't believe it,' cried DS Holdsworth, 'it's him or if it isn't him, it's an identical twin brother. But it can't be, can it?'

'Who are we looking at?' exclaimed DS Hodgson feeling slightly left out of it, 'I don't recognise anyone on here.'

'Tim Ridgway! The one who is looking miserable there second on the left? He's only working for the Police in Australia on Project bloody Watchman!' replied the DCI excitedly, 'I'm positive it's him, it has to be. I'd stake my bloody police pension on it'.

Jack Hodgson suddenly remembered the name and the prison escape from his undercover days at HMP Dinas Bay. He stood there feeling slightly foolish that he hadn't even spotted Ridgway on the photograph but sure enough it could be Ridgway.

'Right, now get onto the Project Watchman team, Jack, immediately and check this out,' said the DCI now rubbing his hands, 'with a bit of luck, we can have Ridgway back where he belongs behind bars and I don't mean the drinking ones.'

***

Wednesday, 27 July, 2016

DS Hodgson had set the alarm for 4am and was at his desk just after 5.30 am to ensure that he was in the office bright and early to contact Adam Taylor in Perth. It had been too late to contact him the previous evening and to be honest, he was still personally not convinced the man in the photograph was in fact Tim Ridgway. The office was empty as expected when he made the phone call to Police HQ in Perth.

'Good afternoon, Project Watchman, Adam Taylor speaking.'

'Ah, good afternoon, Adam. This is DS Jack Hodgson calling from Midshire Police, we spoke last week.'

'Hello Jack, yes it's good to hear from you. Did you find the information pack that we sent useful?'

'Erm yes, Adam, it was very useful indeed. But you might find this a little odd. But there is a photograph in the pack of your development team and I wonder if you could confirm that you have someone there called Tim Ridgway, I believe he's one of your programmers?'

'No, we have no one of that name, I have the photograph right here. Which person is it that you are referring to?'

'The second one from the left, he seems to be the only one on there not smiling.'

'Ah yes, that's Paul Arrowsmith. He doesn't work directly for us. He's a contract programmer from CCI who had won the contract to help us on the development of Phases 1 and 2. He is off sick at present but I can give you CCI's contact details if you like. The company is run by a Mr Richard Ashcroft, an ex-police officer from here.'

Jack Hodgson looked again at the photograph, he thought it could be him and of course he had been likely to change his name.

'Yes, if you could, Adam. That would be great.'

Adam then provided Jack with the contact details for Richard Ashcroft at CCI.

'Adam, can I ask you not to say anything about this phone call to anyone and certainly not to Paul Arrowsmith, it's just a precaution. I'm sure you understand. I'll be in touch.'

'Yes of course, Jack, mums the word. Bye for now.'

Adam Taylor replaced the receiver and sat back thinking to himself that it had been strange, he'd noticed that Paul Arrowsmith had been acting odd recently.

***

Friday, 29 July, 2016

Kevin McNeil was excited for once, he thought at last this could be the cross roads that he'd been waiting for, a fresh start in life. He was watching the clock all morning and eventually decided to drive over to Kewdale a little earlier than needed as he wasn't quite sure of the actual location of the warehouse. In hindsight, it was a good job he did leave early as it took him some considerable time to get through the lunchtime traffic.

He drove through the small industrial estate which seemed to be run down in parts with a number of the units displaying *For Lease* and *For Sale* signs. Eventually, he found what he was looking for, a large warehouse Unit 17 which was set back from all the others. It too had a *For Lease* sign screwed to the front wall of what looked to have been a small adjacent office block. The building looked in desperate need of a fresh coat of paint and there was graffiti scrawled across the heavy metal shutters which were padlocked down on all the windows. The place looked completely deserted.

He was unsure at first whether he'd even got the right address. It certainly didn't look impressive enough to offer an exciting business opportunity as described in the mysterious letter. He stopped and double checked the letter, yes it was definitely correct. He parked the car on the roadway and walked over to the front door and rang the doorbell. He waited for about five minutes and decided to try the door handle, which he expected to be locked but surprisingly it opened. There wasn't a sign of anyone and the building looked as though it hadn't been used for some considerable time. The front door opened into a small waiting room which had a strange musty smell of stale tobacco and coffee. Piles of junk mail and old local newspapers had been strewn across the floor. A small hatchway presumably through to the warehouse was locked from the inside. He pushed open a side door which took him into a small reception office. Apart from a small notice board, which displayed an old health and safety notice, the room was almost empty. Near the door leading to the warehouse, there were just a couple of orange plastic chairs stacked in the corner. He was reluctant to go any further and stood there for a moment waiting for someone to arrive.

After five minutes, he decided to venture through the door leading into the large warehouse area. It was completely deserted all except for a stand-alone notice board at the far end, which seemed to have a number of posters neatly pinned to it. He was curious and as he got nearer he could see they weren't posters after all but photographs. There must have been over twenty photographs of a young family at a number of different events, on holiday, on the beach, enjoying Christmas dinner and playing in the garden. They all looked happy and enjoying themselves. He didn't recognise any of them, why should he. He thought it odd but they must have been left here from the previous occupants, presumably having some form of family reunion party before the warehouse closed.

As he was studying each one of them, he hadn't noticed that a young man had crept quietly into the warehouse and was now standing immediately behind him. Just as he sensed someone was there and before he could even turn around, a sackcloth bag was pulled over his head and tied tight at the neck. He struggled to remove the bag but it was futile, as he turned, he lost his balance and was kicked to the ground. Before he knew it, he was lying on the floor with his legs and hands bound with duct tape. He could now hear his assailant breathing heavily and catching his breath back. He then found himself being dragged across the dusty warehouse floor. With the sacking over his head, Kevin McNeil was now struggling to breath. Just as he thought he was going to pass out, he felt a blade of a knife pass over the hessian cloth just enough for an air hole by his mouth. He managed to take in large gulps of stale air through the hessian sacking.

'Who are you,' he pleaded, 'let me go, please what do you want?'

For one moment, Kevin McNeil assumed he was being kidnapped. He would now be held for a ransom, possibly by someone who hadn't realised that the millionaire was now almost penniless.

'Please, let me go, who are you?'

'Oh, you'll find out who I am, all in good time. All in good time,' he repeated, 'we don't want to rush this, do we? Do you know I've waited years for this? So I'm not going to hurry it now, not for you or anyone. I'm going to savour it. I've dreamt about this moment and now it's here I'm going to enjoy every single minute of it. I've rehearsed this in my mind so many times, every single step of it.'

Kevin thought he recognised the voice but he still couldn't quite place it. It was familiar somehow. The accent was definitely familiar to him.

'Look, if its money you are after, I haven't got any money. I'm broke, I've lost everything. Please let me go whoever you are.'

There was a further moment of heavy breathing as his assailant worked through the next steps in his mind.

'Did you enjoy the photo gallery, Mr McNeil? I noticed you showed a lot of interest in it. They were quite a nice young family. I'm sure you'll agree, just like the nice young family you used to have. Well that was my family. That was all I had, all I had in the world apart from my dear old grandmother of course, who looked after me. God bless her soul.'

'Who are you, what do you want of me, let me go?'

'Well let's see now, you might remember me as Mr Greene. Do you remember Mr V. Greene, Kevin? Mr Greene in the

Government Procurements department?' he laughed out loudly, 'Well that was me, I'm Mr V. Greene, of course that's not my real name. In fact I've almost forgotten my real name, isn't that strange. No V. Greene it's an anagram of revenge, good eh. I've been watching you, Kevin. Oh yes I've followed your every move. Nowhere was safe, even inside your house. Oh how I've waited for this moment!'

Kevin McNeil now remembered the voice on the telephone.

'I've enjoyed our little conversations on the phone and I'm sure you didn't mind me ringing you early in the morning to tell you that your warehouse was on fire. Yes, it was me all along and you fell for it hook, line and sinker even going straight over to view the place. Not a bad ozzy accent was it? I'd make a good police officer, don't you think? And of course, we mustn't forget your lovely beautiful landscaped garden overgrown with weeds, I imagine, now without a proper gardener to look after it, pity. I would have enjoyed working there even though I know sod all about bloody gardening.'

Yes, Kevin now remembered the would-be gardener coming to see him. The young man who applied for the vacancy and then didn't turn up for duty having then been offered the job. This was the same person, the same voice.

'And I suppose you must have been the person who sabotaged the laptops in the warehouse?' mumbled Kevin who was struggling to speak through the hessian sack cloth.

'Ah, yes the laptops, strange that one. I read about that in the newspaper, but no I'm so sorry to tell you that wasn't me but just wished I'd thought of it. It appears you have more than one enemy, Mr McNeil and why am I not surprised.'

It still didn't make sense to Kevin McNeil what was going on here. It was like a bad dream but just then he was dragged onto a chair and bound up. The rope was so tight now it was cutting into Kevin McNeil's arms. He couldn't move, he was now tied to the chair which was pushed against the warehouse wall and was quite simply helpless. Suddenly, it had gone quiet, deathly quiet, *Perhaps he's gone,* he thought. But then all he could hear was footsteps walking off in the distance.

He sat there in the darkness with the minutes ticking by, which seemed more like hours and then suddenly, the silence was broken. He could hear one of the warehouse doors being cranked open. The heavy metal doors sounded as though they hadn't been open for some considerable time as the shutters grinded slowly open. *At last*, he thought, *someone is coming to release me and this nightmare will all be over soon.*

He then heard a car engine starting up outside and it sounded as if it was being driven inside the warehouse. The heavy metal door of the warehouse was cranked closed and the next thing he heard was the car engine revving up. He panicked as he sat there completely helpless. Was it his imagination that the car seemed to be getting nearer and then reversing, taunting him, testing him? Over and over again, getting just that bit closer then reversing back, each time getting nearer, faster and louder. It was pointless crying out; no one would hear him anyway.

He sat there waiting, his breathing becoming heavier. He could hear the car engine ticking over at the far end of the warehouse. It was silent. Seconds later, he heard the car now coming towards him gathering great speed. The next thing he felt was the sheer blinding pain and the cracking sound of bones splintering in his legs as the car hit him full on, the impact knocking him firmly against the wall. The car reversed a few metres back and then revved up again. He passed out with the pain, what sort of mindless person would do this to another human being.

When he eventually came round, the pain in his legs was completely off the scale but he was now also wary of someone now standing directly over him.

'It hurts doesn't it? So are you going to apologise to me now or shall we have another go? I quite enjoyed that,' came the voice out of the darkness.

'Apologise for what, I've done nothing. Who are you and what is it that I'm supposed to have done?'

'What, you haven't a clue, have you? You don't even remember, well maybe this will help you,' taunted the voice as the ball hammer shattered what was left of Kevin McNeil's right kneecap.

Kevin wept with the pain. He had never felt such excruciating pain like this.

'It's not nice, is it having a car run into you. So are you going to apologise now for what you did all those years ago back on that street in Manchester? You killed my parents, you bloody bastard, and then drove off,' said Paul Arrowsmith, 'you left them to die, left them to bloody well die at the side of the road. Well it's my turn now as I'm going to leave you to die and let's see how you like it.'

'I'm sorry, I'm really sorry. Please let me go,' Kevin pleaded, 'I was a different person then. Yes, I do remember the incident and you must forgive me please for what I did. I was wrong, I was young and foolish and this has lived with me all of my life. Please, please let me go and call me an ambulance, please.'

***

Sergeant Rod Kelly opened his emails to find that the Watchman report he'd asked for was already sitting in his email inbox. He'd previously submitted the date and time range of the incident and within minutes, he'd received an automated document consisting of several pages and images. With the time range in the middle of the night, it was of course quieter than normal. However, there were several sightings of people walking their dogs, coming home from nightclubs etc. before retiring home for the evening. The vehicle recognition module had provided a number of vehicle registrations and there was a clear view of the blue Nissan Micra that had been sighted around midnight. The automated registration look up had shown it belonged to a hire company in East Perth. But it was the facial recognition module which had been working overtime and it had also picked out the face of the driver at the traffic lights just down from the warehouse.

Sergeant Kelly immediately reached for the phone and called his boss, Inspector Wolfe.

'Boss, we have something of interest here from Project Watchman that I think you should look at.'

'I'm a bit tied up at present, Rod. What is it?'

'Well we now have a positive identification of the vehicle at midnight just outside the warehouse gates, it belongs to a local hire company.'

'Well that's better than nothing I suppose, we should at least be able to trace the hirer,' responded the inspector.

‘Yes but it’s better than that, boss. There’s more, we have a photograph of the driver and the facial recognition has matched it against the database, actually our own database. Guess what, he’s only one of ours, he’s a bloody civilian working at Police Headquarters!’

***

Kevin McNeil had passed out with the excruciating pain. He was now bent over but still sitting in the chair on the warehouse floor. When he eventually came round, he could hear someone sobbing uncontrollably in the far corner. He had no idea how long he’d been there. He still couldn’t see through the hessian sack which was still tied tightly over his head. He guessed it must now be early evening, but he had no real idea of time.

The sobbing continued and then suddenly, he heard a voice in the darkness.

‘Why, why did you do it? You ruined my sodding life, you bloody bastard.’

But Kevin could do nothing. He decided not to speak back, but just had to sit there through the intense pain and listen to the crying and wailing coming from the corner.

Just then he heard footsteps and the car engine starting up.

He thought, *Please god, no more, I can’t take anymore.* But he could now hear the warehouse doors opening and the car driving out. There was nothing now, nothing but silence except for the rain now beating incessantly down on the corrugated metal roof and the cold winter wind, which was now starting to howl through the open doorway.

Chapter 21

Saturday, 30 July, 2016

Paul Arrowsmith aka Tim Ridgway had raced back to his apartment in South Perth. He'd previously packed his bags and his plan was now almost complete. All that remained now was for him to leave Australia as quickly as possible and head to the Far East. He had no intention of returning to the warehouse, his work yesterday was done. Kevin McNeil could rot in hell, as far as he was concerned, why did he care. Somebody would find him eventually and that was the least of his concerns, for now he just wanted to leave the country. As far as he was concerned, he'd done what he'd set out to do. All those years, he'd sat working out his plan of revenge. It had taken years and all had gone to plan, better in fact.

Not only that he had finally caught up with the driver who had run down and killed both his parents but also he'd managed to take the revenge out on his business. It was now time for a fresh start with a new identity. He'd booked his business class airline ticket on the early morning flight to Hong Kong and arranged for an old friend and business acquaintance Chung Lee to meet him there. He'd arranged for the hire car to be left at Perth airport so everything was now in place for his new start in life. He found it strange that Tariq Atiq had suddenly stopped communicating with him on the closed Facebook group, but he assumed that the tablet had been confiscated in the prison. In any case, he had access to the bitcoin account from all the ransomware attacks.

He drove to the airport, parked the car in the hire car bay, handed over the keys at the car hire desk and checked in for the eight-hour flight. The business lounge was very quiet and he virtually had the place to himself. He poured himself a glass of bucks fizz from the bar and walked over to the cold buffet. He was now feeling a bit peckish having missed breakfast at his apartment. He started to fill his plate with croissants and hadn't noticed the three business men in suits arrive immediately after him in the lounge.

'Good morning, Tim, we meet again.'

Tim turned round and dropped his plate on the floor. He was about to run for the door but it was now being blocked by two burly airport security officers.

'It's good to see you again, Tim,' said DS Holdsworth 'well, well fancy finding you here. Can I introduce you to DCI Bentley? We've come a long way to find you and we are a bit jet lagged but it's been worth it. You can get to know each other a bit better on the flight back to the UK. Tim Ridgway, you are now under arrest after escaping from HMP Dinas Bay. You do not have to say anything. But, it may harm your defence if you do not mention when questioned something, which you later rely on in court. Anything you do say may be given in evidence.'

Tim Ridgway was silent and in a state of shock.

'Oh, how rude of me. Please forgive me, I haven't introduced you to this other gentleman. This is Inspector Wolfe from Fremantle Police who also has a few questions to ask you first.'

Tim knew the game was up, it was futile trying to resist arrest. Minutes later, he was bundled into the back of a police car heading for his office at Police HQ, but this time he would be using a different entrance.

***

WA Courier – Sunday, 31 July, 2016

A 58 year old man was recovering in hospital today in a critical condition and is being treated for severe injuries. Emergency services were called to a deserted warehouse in Kewdale yesterday morning after some children who were playing in the area discovered business man Kevin McNeil who was found tied and bound. A 26 year old man is helping police with their enquiries.

***

Tim Ridgway (also known as Paul Arrowsmith), a contract programmer working on the controversial government project known as Watchman was yesterday remanded in custody after appearing in Perth Central Court charged with arson, breaking and entering and grievous bodily harm with intent.

Ridgway aged 26 years was on the run having escaped from HMP Dinas Bay in North Wales, UK earlier this year.

***

Epilogue

A multi-million dollar experimental project was finally wound up today after a judgement at a High Court Tribunal stated that government agencies had broken the law by scooping sensitive information without sufficient oversight or supervision. Project Watchman had harvested and stored data from a number of sources to aid and streamline crime investigations across the state. The tribunal stated that although Watchman had been responsible for assisting with the detection of a number of high profile cases, the actions had breached human rights laws.

Frank Carstairs who had led the protest group BBWatchman and had openly protested for months against Project Watchman said today, "It was a triumph for common sense but it was a shame that so much of tax payers' money had been wasted in finally reaching this decision."

An appeal by the investigative agencies has been scheduled for later this year.